More Greatness →

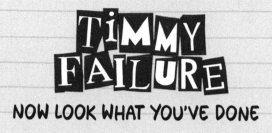

NOW LOOK WHAT YOU'VE DONE

TIMMY FAILURE

NOW LOOK WHAT YOU'VE DONE

STEPHAN PASTIS

CANDLEWICK PRESS

Copyright © 2014 by Stephan Pastis
Timmy Failure font copyright © 2012 by Stephan Pastis

First edition 2014

Library of Congress Catalog Card Number 2013944145
ISBN 978-0-7636-6051-2

13 14 15 16 17 18 BVG 10 9 8 7 6 5 4 3 2 1

Printed in Berryville, VA, U.S.A.

This book was typeset in Nimrod.
The illustrations were done in pen and ink.

Candlewick Press
99 Dover Street
Somerville, Massachusetts 02144

visit us at www.candlewick.com

Visit www.timmyfailure.com
for games, downloadables, activities,
a blog, and more!

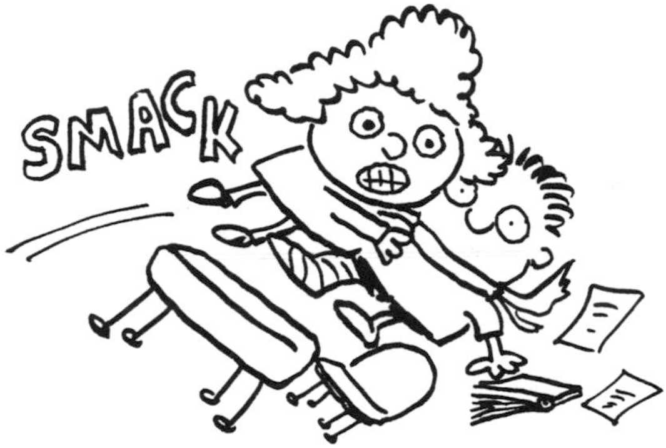
SMACK

A Prologue That Will Most Likely Make Sense Later

Of all the items that can clog your plumbing, an overweight Arctic mammal is probably the worst.

Because while a good plumber can clear your pipes of a spoon or a hair ball or a bar of soap, it is much harder to remove one of these:

That, you see, is a polar bear.

And today he is stuck in a different kind of pipe.

The Tube O' Terror.

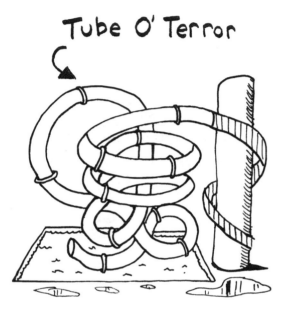

The Tube O' Terror is the world's fastest, curviest waterslide.

But it is not fast today.

Because it is clogged.

Clogged by an overeager polar bear who was much too plump to ride.

And yet somebody let him.

And that is where the bribery comes in.

Because a polar bear who fails to get his way will charm. And a polar bear who fails to charm will deceive. And a polar bear who fails to deceive will grab a big wad of dollar bills from his pocket and wink.

Because that is how the world works.

And then this will happen.

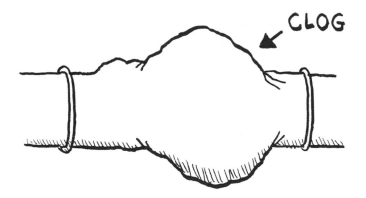

And if you are a world-class detective who just so happens to be tied to that polar bear and had no choice but to follow him down the slide, you are in trouble.

Deep, unbreathable trouble.

Because the rushing water keeps coming.

And with the polar bear's big bottom acting as a plug, the water has nowhere to go but back up the tube.

Which is where I am.

Trapped underwater.

And not very happy about it.

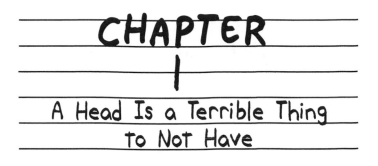

CHAPTER 1

A Head Is a Terrible Thing to Not Have

Carl Kobalinski is not the smartest person in the world.

But try telling that to the woman in the checkered vest.

"Maury's Museum of World Records is now closed," she says. "And you need to go home."

"But look at this thing," I tell her. "It's an outrage."

"What is?" she asks.

"This," I say, pointing directly at the statue.

"Kid, I get eight dollars an hour to walk around this museum and make sure no one breaks anything. If you have a problem with what's in it, tell someone else."

"I've got a problem, all right. Lies, lies, and more lies. Everyone knows who the smartest person is."

"Wonderful," she mumbles, rubbing her temples.

"It's me," I say.

"Good for you," she says, pushing me toward the exit with one hand. "Now let me show the smartest person in the world how a door works."

I am suddenly tempted to pull rank.

Reveal that I am this guy:

Timmy Failure

Distinctive scarf

It is a name so recognizable that she would instantly know it as that of the founder, president, and CEO of the greatest detective agency in the town, probably the state. Perhaps the nation.

But I don't pull rank.

I do something smarter.

I climb Carl Kobalinski and try to yank down his sign.

"What do you think you're doing?" screams the museum woman.

"I'm saving the credibility of your institution!" I retort.

But I'm not.

Because I can't reach the sign without jumping. And I am nine feet above the ground.

So I do what only the smartest person in the world would think to do.

I jump.

Only to learn that while Carl may have had a strong brain, his statue does not have a strong neck.

And as I jump, it snaps. Sending both me and Carl's overrated head tumbling.

Me →

Carl's Overrated Head

Straight to the museum floor.

Where I hear another snap.

This one in my leg.

And say the only logical thing I can to the museum woman leaning over me:

"Now look what you've done."

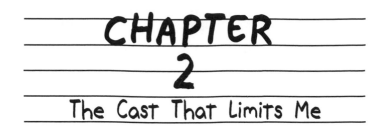

CHAPTER 2

The Cast That Limits Me

When you're lying in bed with a broken right leg, you can either cry or write your memoirs.

And Timmy Failure doesn't cry.

So here are my memoirs:

I was born.

I exhibited greatness.

I founded an empire.

And that empire was achieved despite the many obstacles around me.

Such as Obstacle No. 1.

That's my mother.

She's a kind enough person. But she has her weaknesses.

Like insisting I attend this place:

Now, school is fine for those who need it.

But for those touched by greatness, it is a debilitating nuisance.

Then there's Obstacle No. 2.

His name is Total. He is a fifteen-hundred-pound polar bear.

He was raised in the Arctic. But his home melted like an ice cube in the sun. And he wandered 3,000 or so miles to my house.

So I gave him a job.

And for the first six months, he was the most reliable polar bear I've ever employed.

Then he revealed his true colors.

It was a betrayal so profound that I do not wish to discuss it.

So let me just say this.

If a polar bear ever works very hard for you in the first six months of employment, keep this one thing in mind:

IT IS A RUSE.

Do NOT make him a partner at your detective agency.

Do NOT agree to change the name of the agency from "Failure, Inc." to "Total Failure, Inc."

And, hey, while I'm issuing warnings, do NOT model your life after the person who is Obstacle No. 3.

His name is Rollo Tookus. He is my best friend. And he is boring.

Boring because all he cares about is grades.

So that's all the description he gets.

And I will fill the space he otherwise would have gotten in these memoirs with a drawing of my face.

CHAPTER 3

Drags Like Butter

When you are one of the world's high-profile detectives, you can expect your fair share of high-profile cases.

And the one I get this morning on the Timmyline is about as high profile as it gets.

The call is from a classmate. Nunzio Benedici.

And he is missing something precious.

"I can't find Spooney Spoon," he says.

"Don't panic," I tell him. "I'll be there in twenty."

And I don't necessarily mean minutes. It could be hours.

Because of this thing I've had on my leg the past couple weeks.

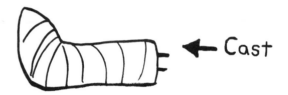

← Cast

Which means I can't walk fast.

Now, that wouldn't have been a problem when I had the Failuremobile.

← Failuremobile

That was a Segway I borrowed from my mother.

But then my mother sold it.

So then I had the Totalmobile.

Totalmobile

That was a wagon pulled by my business partner.

But then my mother sold it (the wagon, not the business partner).

So now I just let my business partner drag me through the streets on a rope.

Which may seem difficult.

But it's not.

Because I coat myself in butter.

So now I have the Buttermobile.

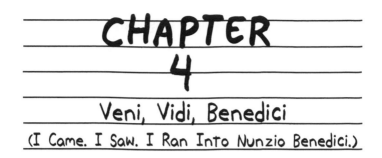

CHAPTER 4

Veni, Vidi, Benedici

(I Came. I Saw. I Ran Into Nunzio Benedici.)

As if I need to tell you, Nunzio Benedici is the kid in my class who can shove the most eraser tips in his nose.

← Nunzio Benedici

And Spooney Spoon is the spoon he uses to eat his applesauce.

Spooney Spoon

Don't ask me why there's a dog's head on it. I don't know.

And I won't ask.

Because if there's one thing you learn in this business, it's that clients have their secrets. Each more shameful than the last.

So when I arrive at his house, I stick to the basics.

"Prepare for a three-month investigation," I tell him. "And perhaps some international travel."

"International travel?" he replies.

Naive clients. The bane of a detective's existence.

"Spoon Larceny 101, kid. When a spoon goes missing, the first thing they do is ship it over the border."

"I didn't know," he says.

"There's a lot you don't know," I tell him. "That's what you pay me for."

"How much will it be?" he asks.

"Four dollars a day. Plus expenses."

"Expenses?" he asks as he reaches into his pocket for change.

But as he does, he sneezes.

And I am hit by a hundred eraser tips.

"Dry-cleaning my scarf," I say. "Your first expense."

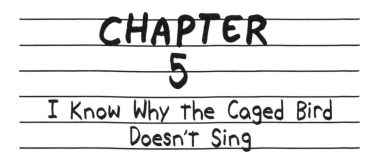

CHAPTER 5

I Know Why the Caged Bird Doesn't Sing

Eraser tips are not the only menace in my life these days.

There is also my great-aunt.

Who right now seems far from great.

I say that because she has attached wheels to her shoes and run into the birdcage.

And now she's unconscious.

I'd help her, but it's the second time today.

And fourth time this week.

Which is something I know because I live with her.

I suppose I should explain.

My mother, my polar bear, and I used to live in an apartment. But my mother lost her job.

So we had to move in with my mother's aunt Colander.

A colander is the thing you use to drain spaghetti.

Colander

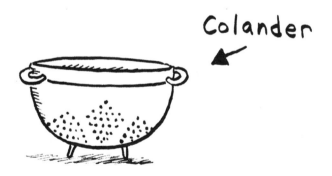

I'm not sure how she got that name.

Perhaps it is because she has holes in her head through which her brain cells escape.

Brain cells

All I know for sure is that she once had a husband, Great-Uncle Gustav.

Gustav

But then he died. Possibly to escape Great-Aunt Colander.

GUSTAV
R.I.P.

Escaped

But Gustav was rich. And when he died, he left my mother's aunt with a big mansion in the big-mansion-filled town of Santa Marinara.

Now, that should be enough for any great-aunt. But it's not.

Not enough ↙

Because Great-Aunt Colander believes she has not yet made her contribution to the civilized world.

That, she believes, is this:

← THE BOOM BOOM SHOEWHEEL

The Boom Boom Shoewheel is a set of two wheels that you attach to each of your shoes.

It is not a roller skate.

The difference, as Great-Aunt Colander will explain to you for the better part of an afternoon, is that a roller skate *already comes with a shoe.*

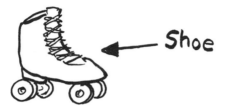 Shoe

The Boom Boom Shoewheel does not.

 No Shoe

That is apparently too subtle a distinction for sporting-goods stores, all of whom refuse to carry this dangerous product and refuse to take any more phone calls from Great-Aunt Colander.

I only wish *I* could get away from her that easily.

But I can't.

So the best I can do is enjoy some of the perks that come with a mansion.

Like the fact that my detective agency is now housed in its largest office to date.

My great-aunt's solarium.

It's spacious. It has great views. And the glass offers protection.

Against the wind.

The bees.

And the occasional flying aunt.

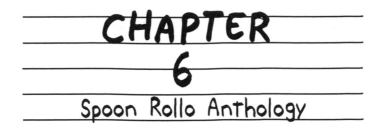

CHAPTER 6

Spoon Rollo Anthology

Flying aunts or no flying aunts, the Nunzio Benedici case will not wait.

So I have traveled again to Nunzio's house. And I'm conducting a lineup.

"Stand still," I say to Rollo Tookus. "This is official police business."

"I have a book report due," says Rollo.

"And don't talk," I tell him. "It's distracting."

I turn to Nunzio.

"Okay, Nunzio. Is this the fellow you saw take your favorite spoon? The one you call Spooney Spoon?"

"Rollo?" says Nunzio. "Of course not. All he ever does is study."

I make a note of that in my detective log.

I look back at Nunzio.

"So if I understand you correctly, you think Rollo took Spooney Spoon."

"That's not what I said," says Nunzio.

"Well, I wish you would," I say. "He's the only guy I could get to come over."

"That does it," says Rollo. "I'm going home."

"Look what you've done," I yell at Rollo. "You've intimidated the witness."

"I'm not intimidated," says Nunzio.

"Fine," I tell him. "We have more suspects to go through anyway."

But we don't.

So I grab anyone I can to parade in front of Nunzio.

"Is this the fellow you saw take your favorite spoon?"

"I keep telling you," says Nunzio. "I didn't see anyone take Spooney Spoon."

"Good," I say. "It gets complicated if I have to arrest my own business partner."

"Look," says Nunzio. "For the last time, all I know is that Spooney Spoon is missing."

"All right, all right, calm down," I tell him.

"I am calm," he says. "You're the one who's sweating all over my bedroom carpet."

I laugh with confidence.

"The CEO of the nation's finest detective agency doesn't sweat, Nunzio."

"Then what do you call that?" he says, pointing at my forehead.

"Butter," I say. "Lots and lots of butter."

CHAPTER 7

One Flew Out of the Cuckoo's Nest

Even quick-witted professionals such as myself need time to solve international heists.

But Spooney Spoon will have to wait.

Because of another flying distraction.

My great-aunt's lovebird.

Torpedo Bob.

← TORPEDO BOB

Torpedo Bob was named for his reported propensity to escape from his oft-damaged cage and dive-bomb random targets with a malicious intensity rarely seen outside of war.

And right now, his cage is empty.

← EMPTY

"Darn it, Timmy. I don't have time for this," says my mother. "I have a job interview in ten minutes."

"Get Great-Aunt Colander to find him," I tell her. "It's her fault for always crashing into the cage."

"And how am I supposed to do that?" my mom asks, pointing at the unconscious Great-Aunt Colander.

Unconscious

"So help me look for the silly bird," says
my mom.

But I can't.

Because the Total Failure Alert goes off.

The Total Failure Alert is a high-tech
alarm system developed by Total Failure, Inc.,
labs to warn agency personnel of impending
doom.

It consists of three sandwich baggies.

Three
baggies

A set of these is distributed to each Total Failure employee upon completion of basic training. (Known as Achieving Baggie Privileges.)

While the manner in which a threatened employee utilizes the alert is both highly technical and legally patented, I shall try to explain it here:

Employee fills baggies.

Employee pops baggies.

But don't get bogged down in the technical details.

Because the important part is this.

An employee may **ONLY** sound the alert when one of two life-threatening situations is happening:

      1. the world is ending; or

      2. the WEDGIE is present.

The WEDGIE (face blurred for your protection.)

WEDGIE stands for:

Worldwide
Enemy of
Da
Goodness
In
Everything.

And she is just as uncomfortable as that other kind of wedgie.

Narrator's demonstration of that other kind of wedgie *

* Extreme variety wherein underwear is pulled up so far it can be stretched over head.

In her long and sordid past, the Wedgie has gone by many nicknames (the Beast, the Evil One, the Weevil Bun). But I'm not going to go into it.

Because we're not going to talk about her.

Suffice it to say that when I hear the Total Failure Alert, I know it can only have come from one individual:

My business partner.

And wherever he is, he is in trouble.

Life-threatening trouble.

So I hobble toward the sound of the alert.
Down a long hallway. Up a flight of stairs.
Through an arched doorway.
Into old Gustav's study.
Where I find this guy:

Hiding from this guy:

Meaning that this guy:

Has lost his Baggie Privileges.

CHAPTER 8

When the Moon Hits Your Eye

Mr. Jenkins is making an announcement.

He is my teacher.

ANNOUNCEMENTS

But I'm not listening.

Mostly because I am taping Rollo Tookus to his desk.

"What are you doing?" he whines. "I want to hear what he's saying. It sounds interesting."

"School is never interesting," I say, preparing to tape down his free hand.

"But he's announcing a contest," he says.

"And I'm doing a science project. I call it Our Friendly Universe."

"Can I please hear this?" he says.

"Now, listen," I tell him. "You're the sun. So you're stationary. Hence, all the tape."

"Oh, great. He just said the deadline. And I didn't hear it."

"And I'm the earth," I continue. "So I'll circle you like I'm in orbit, though that could be difficult with a broken leg."

I limp around Rollo to demonstrate my orbit.

"You're blocking my view," he says.

"Do you mind if I paint you orange?" I ask him.

"Paint me *what*?" Rollo says.

"I want to play!" squeals a girl.

It is Molly Moskins. The girl who ruins everything.

← MOLLY MOSKINS
(Ruins everything.)

The reason she ruins everything is that she smiles too much and she smells like a tangerine.

Plus, she has one pupil that is bigger than the other and has no respect for personal space.

"Give us room, Molly Moskins. I'm on the verge of a Nobel Prize."

But she doesn't give us room. She runs closely around me.

"What are you doing?" I yell.

"I'm the moon!" she chirps. "And I run around you while you circle around Rollo."

"Will you two please shut up?" asks Rollo.

"That's absurd," I say to Molly. "For one thing, you're carrying a Hello Catty lunch box. The moon would never carry a Hello Catty lunch box."

I try to push her away while I limp around Rollo.

"I love my Hello Catty lunch box!" she shouts as she waltzes around me.

"I'm getting dizzy," cries Rollo.

"WHEEEEE!" cheers Molly Moskins, now running with her eyes closed.

"I'm getting nauseous," complains Rollo.

"What do you three think you're doing?" barks Mr. Jenkins.

Whose voice surprises the moon.

Who runs right out of her orbit and into the sun.

Who falls on the earth.

Who careens into a storage closet.

The entire universe has collapsed.

"Well, I hope you're happy," I tell Mr. Jenkins. "You've discouraged three kids who were otherwise very interested in science."

CHAPTER 9

Ousters and Insults and Bears — Oh, My!

"All in favor of ousting the bear from the board, please raise your hand."

I raise mine.

Total does not.

We are at loggerheads.

This is how all the board meetings of Total Failure, Inc., go.

The only difference now is that we hold the meetings in a huge room. My great-aunt's dining room.

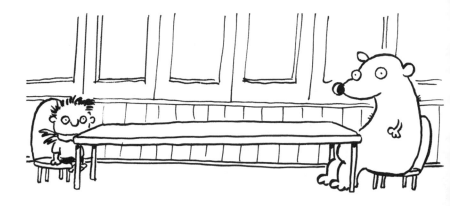

"You're lazy. You're a glutton. And you run from small birds," I tell him.

This is how all our meetings end. With personal insults.

Total leans back to reply. But his chair collapses.

"And how many times do I have to tell you not to lean back in that chair? You're a thousand pounds over its capacity."

My mother barges in from the kitchen.

"Blame the bear," I tell her.

"Did Aunt Colander say you could play in here?"

"No one's *playing*. It's a board meeting. And if you interrupt again, I'll have to ask my security detail over there to escort you out."

I point at Total.

Total yawns.

"Timmy, why didn't you show this to me?" she asks, holding up a piece of paper.

"I don't even know what it is. But if you're going to interrupt the meeting, you could at least say, 'Point of order.'"

"Point of order, then. It's a notice from your school. It was in your backpack."

"You're rifling through my papers? At long last, ma'am, have you no sense of decency?"

"It says that the school's holding a detective contest. You should enter."

I grab the sheet of paper from her hand.

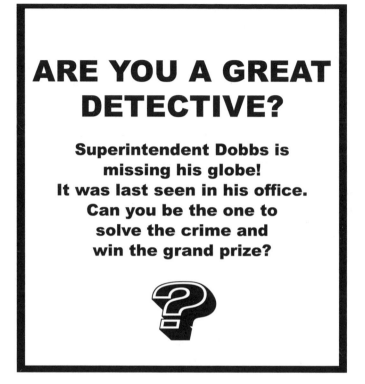

ARE YOU A GREAT DETECTIVE?

Superintendent Dobbs is missing his globe! It was last seen in his office. Can you be the one to solve the crime and win the grand prize?

"Is this a farce?" I ask.

"It's a contest, Timmy. It sounds fun."

"Fun? It's a personal insult. They *know* who the greatest detective is."

"Nobody's trying to insult you, Timmy. It's just a game."

"It's not a game, Mother. It's a direct shot at me, the agency, and my global reputation."

"Oh, my goodness," she says, leaving the room. "I'm sorry I showed it to you."

Total follows her out. The gluttonous bear follows anyone who walks into the kitchen.

"This slander shall not go unanswered!" I declare to the boardroom. "All in favor of proving that Timmy Failure is nobody's fool?"

But the room is empty.

So nobody seconds my motion.

"Motion passes," I declare.

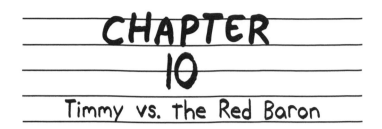

CHAPTER 10
Timmy vs. the Red Baron

Principal Scrimshaw's office is a serious place.
So I have worn a serious hat.

"Timmy, I don't know what to tell you," he says. "It's a contest. No one's making fun of you."

But I can't hear him.

Because my hat came with a biplane that circles around it.

RRRRRRRRRRRRR

"You'll have to speak up," I tell him. "The plane is loud."

"It's a contest!" he shouts. "No one's making fun of you!"

The plane recedes behind my head.

"Relax," I say. "You can talk normally now."

"Timmy, I have a lot of things to do. If you want to enter, enter. Your submission needs to be into this office on Friday. My secretary, Marilyn, can give you the exact time."

"Absurd," I reply. "That's three days from now. I can solve your mystery right now."

"Yeah, well, it's not *my* mystery. It's the district's. So you'll be competing against entries from all of the other schools as well. And whoever turns in the most well-written and thorough solution will win."

"How sad for the other students," I say. "Do they know that they're competing against a professional?"

"I don't know what they know, Timmy," he says, putting on his suit jacket. "But you need to go, because the teachers and I have our monthly meeting with the superintendent."

"Just one more thing," I say.

"Hurry," he says, stopping in the doorway.

"I think we both know that I bring

tremendous star power to your contest. So the question is obvious. What's in it for me?"

"Oh, good gosh," he says. "I'm leaving. Marilyn, see that he leaves my office."

His secretary walks in. She smiles.

Marilyn,
the Smiling
Secretary

"All that money's not enough for you, Timmy?"

"What are you talking about?"

"I'm sorry," she says. "I couldn't help eavesdropping. The winner gets money."

"The winning detective gets money?"

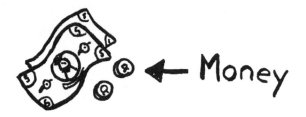
← Money

"Yep," she says.

"How much?"

"Five hundred dollars."

"Five hundred *dollars*? That's a fortune!"

"Well. No. But it's a lot."

"The agency could go global! I could open that office in Peru!"

"I like your enthusiasm," she says.

"This isn't about enthusiasm. It's about the start of an *empire*."

"I see," she says.

"With Timmy Failure at its head!"

"Wonderful!" she says.

"Because Timmy Failure is nobody's fool!" I shout.

To which she says something something something something.

None of which I hear.

Because the biplane comes back.

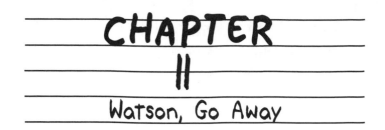

CHAPTER 11

Watson, Go Away

Holding hands is the second worst thing in the world.

The worst is holding hands with this person.

"I'm not even supposed to be using this leg," I shout.

"I see you hobbling around on it all the time," replies my great-aunt.

"Mendacity!" I shout.

"Mendacity!" she repeats. "I like that word."

"I should be in bed right now. Recuperating."

"No, you shouldn't. You love the museum."

The museum she's talking about is this place:

The same place I got this:

Broken leg

"I wish you had never introduced me to that place," I say. "It's a factory of lies."

"Mendacity!" she shouts, almost losing her balance.

"See why we have to hold hands?" she adds.

"All I know is that Carl Kobalinski is a moron," I tell her.

She grabs on to a passing tree for a rest. "Boom boom stop," she says.

"Boom boom stop" is something she says each time she stops on the Boom Boom Shoewheels. As though holding hands with her isn't embarrassing enough.

"You're probably right," she says.

"Right about what?"

"That Kobalinski fellow. What case did *he* ever solve?"

"Exactly," I say.

"A real genius solves cases," she says. "Like Sherlock Holmes."

"Well, Holmes had his weaknesses," I remind her. "But yes, we detectives are the true geniuses of the world. Which is why I'm about to crack the biggest case of my generation."

"The missing globe?" she asks.

"How'd YOU know about it?"

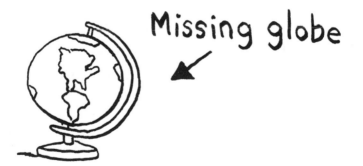

Missing globe

"The flyer. Your mom left it on the dining-room table."

"In plain view?"

"Right next to a broken chair."

"I know nothing," I say.

"Mendacity!" she shouts.

She smiles and begins skating again. This time without the hand-holding.

"I don't care about the chair, Timmy. But I do have an idea."

"What's that?" I ask.

"That Sherlock Holmes fellow. Didn't he have an assistant?

"Watson," I say.

"Watson," she repeats.

"What about him?" I ask.

"Me," she says. "I can be your Watson."

I almost choke on my tongue.

"Absurd," I bark. "You have absolutely no training."

"You could give it to me!"

"Wrong. No chance. I already have an able assistant."

"And who is that?" she asks.

I think of Total. And the last time I saw him. Stealing supplies from the Buttermobile.

"I don't want to discuss it," I tell her.

"Oh, relax," she says. "It was just an idea. Besides, there's the museum."

She points at the block ahead.

But as she does, she loses her balance.

And I grab her hand.

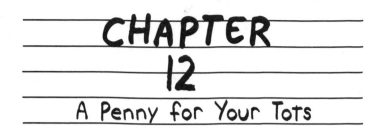

CHAPTER 12

A Penny for Your Tots

It's amateur hour in Kiddieland.

And the pro sits back and sighs.

"What are you doing in the Tater Tot tray?" asks Rollo.

"What are you doing in the cafeteria?" I ask.

"You're the one in the Tater Tot tray."

"It's called *surveillance*. Besides, this sneeze guard offers protection against attack. Now go and play pretend with the other detectives."

"What other detectives?"

"As if you don't know."

"I don't."

"Half this school is running around like bumbling ninnies trying to solve a case they have no hope of solving, and you know nothing about it?"

"You mean the missing globe contest?" he asks. "I'm not doing it."

Finally. A concession to my greatness. I reach under the glass to pat him on the head.

"There, there," I say. "There's no shame in admitting defeat. It's not your fault you were born in the Timmy Failure era."

"I was born in the era of having to get good grades," he says. "And the contest doesn't affect your grade-point average. I asked."

Poor kid. He still thinks grades are important.

Little does he realize how five hundred dollars will set you up for life.

"Yeah, well, you get your good grades,

Rollo. But do me a favor. Be my eyes and ears in this joint. I don't want anyone trying to game the system."

"Game the system?"

"Bamboozle. Hoodwink. Con. Defraud."

"I get it."

"Deceive. Swindle. Sucker. Fleece."

"I get it!" he shouts, shaking his large round head. "I'm just saying I think you're a little paranoid if you think someone's gonna cheat on a school detective contest."

"Paranoid? *Paranoid?* There's not one person in this county, much less this state, who stands a chance against me in this contest. So naturally, I have to guard against the one thing that can bring me down. *Shenanigans.*"

"Shenanigans? Timmy, not everyone has to cheat to beat you."

"Ha!" I yell. "Are you a loon?"

"No, I'm not a loon. I think we both know at least one person in this school who has a chance."

"Say it and you'll ruin my entire day."

"Say what?" asks Rollo.

"I'm telling you, I'll get right on my Buttermobile and leave."

"What are you talking about?"

"The name, Rollo. She Whose Name Shall Not Be Uttered. I don't want it cluttering my large focused brain."

"Ohhh," he says. "You mean Corrina Corrina?"

Name uttered.
Brain cluttered.
Head buttered.

CHAPTER 13

Welcome to the Monkey House

Because big-mouth Rollo opened his big loud
Rollo mouth, you are now going to want to
know all about You-Know-Who.

So fine.

Here you go.

This is Corrina Corrina (aka the Wedgie).

And below is how she is described in our school yearbook. (Feel free to skip over it. It is a cornucopia of lies.)

Corrina Corrina is an honors student and has won a number of academic awards. When she is not in school, she likes to work in her detective agency, the Corrina Corrina Intelligence Agency (CCIA).

The CCIA is headquartered in a former bank building. The building is located downtown and is well stocked with the latest high-tech detective gear!

Corrina Corrina has a good reputation for solving cases and is well liked by her classmates.

Okay. This is me, Timmy, again.

And everything in the above section is a big fat garbanzo lie.

First, not one person likes Corrina Corrina.

Second, she has never solved a case.

And third, she has the ethics of an organ-grinder's monkey.

Organ-GRinder's Monkey

Moreover, a number of pertinent details have been left out. Namely:

- Corrina Corrina is the subject of hundreds of ethics complaints that have been filed with the Better Detective Bureau.[1]
- She is a felon.[2]

---

1. I have filed all of them.
2. She once stole my Failuremobile, though the police claim I parked it in a red zone and got it towed away. That account is pure propaganda.

And last but not least:

- She may be Satan.

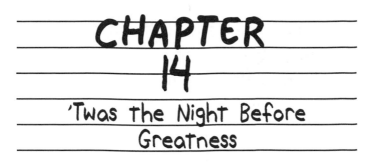

CHAPTER 14

'Twas the Night Before Greatness

It is the night before the contest deadline.

Amateurs everywhere are preparing their entries.

And I am lying in bed designing the Lazy Bear 2000.

"I don't care if you don't like it," I tell my business partner. "Because we're installing it."

The Lazy Bear 2000 is a high-tech device designed by me to monitor my partner's work activity.

It looks like this:

And it works like this:

1. A high-definition camera spies on my business partner.

2. The information from the camera is sent to a computer, which determines whether or not my business partner is being lazy or gluttonous.

3. It also notes when he is being responsible or industrious.

┌   ┐

No photo on file

└   ┘

4. If either of the latter conditions is satisfied, the Lazy Bear 2000 spits out one chicken nugget.

But Total is raising one objection after another.

The product's name.

The invasion of privacy.

The small food portion.

He is also threatening to punch the Lazy Bear 2000 until it spits out *all* of its chicken nuggets.

"It will be made of bear-proof steel," I tell him. "So good luck."

"Good luck with what?" I hear back.

I look up and see my mother. Standing in my bedroom doorway.

"Must you interrupt all my meetings?" I ask.

"The door was open. Besides, our bedrooms are too far apart in this place. I don't like having you so far away from me."

She sits on the edge of the bed and puts her arm around me.

"Finishing your contest entry?" she asks.

"I am not."

"I thought it was due tomorrow."

"It is."

"So you've finished it already?"

Oh, how I yearn for the day when my judgment is no longer questioned by the masses who besiege me.

"I have it under control, Mother. And you're coming very close to outright insulting me."

"No one's insulting you, Timmy. I just know how much this means to you."

She kisses me on the nose and places a peanut-butter cookie in my hand.

"Made them for you," she says, hugging me. "Good luck tomorrow."

"Thank you," I mumble.

And hug her around her neck.

She taps me on the nose with her index finger. "Lights-out in half an hour," she says.

I watch as she closes the door.

And turn back to look at the cookie.

The cookie that is no longer in my hand.

Thanks to a pilfering fur ball.

GLUTTONOUS

CHAPTER
15
By the Time I Get There in My Phoenix

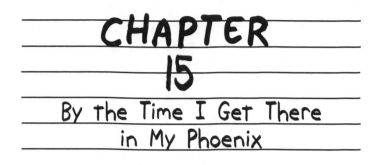

"Can't this thing go any faster?"

"No," says my great-aunt, behind the wheel of her Pontiac Phoenix. "I'm going as fast as I can."

"This thing's gotta be thirty years old!" I tell her. "Why don't you take some of your money and buy a *fast* car?"

"Because I like this one," she says as the car sputters out.

"Fiddlesticks," she says. "Engine always goes kaput on right turns. Know a way to school that only has left turns?"

"What!" I answer as she tries to restart the engine.

But it doesn't respond.

So I hop out.

"What do you think you're doing?" she asks.

"Running for it," I say. "I'm probably five hours late for school as it is!"

"You can't run on a broken leg!"

"I can go faster than this thing," I say, pointing at the broken-down car. "The school's just three blocks away."

I grab my crutch and limp the three blocks as fast as I can.

Which is not very fast.

Because of my banner.

It was essential that I bring it. For it is the motto of my agency.

But it is unwieldy. And eventually the long stretch of cloth becomes wrapped around my head.

And I can't see where I'm going.

And am hit by a train.

"Well, hello, Timmy Failure!" squeals the train that is Molly Moskins. "You ran right into me!"

"Not *now,* Molly Moskins. I'm late!"

"What happened?" she asks.

"My mother didn't wake me! Now, please get off! I have a detective contest to enter!"

But I can see that she's not listening.

Because she's staring at my cast.

"How come you never let me sign that?" she asks.

"Because I didn't let *anybody* sign it! It looks unprofessional! Now, will you *please* get off me?"

But she won't.

Because she is sad.

"Oh, here!" I shout, handing her a piece of chalk I was going to use to color my banner.

Her eyes light up.

"But be quick!" I add, "Because this is the most important day of my life!"

Which it is.

Because today is the day I enter the contest.

And solve the mystery of the missing globe.

And win the money that will enable the agency to expand.

Into places like Peru.

Which seems a long way from where I am now.

Which is facedown on the front lawn of our school while a tangerine-scented girl draws hearts on my leg.

Soon my leg looks like a billboard graf-fitied by Cupid.

"Cute," says Rollo, walking up to us with a half-eaten Pop-Tart hanging from his mouth.

"Don't you have anything better to do?" I shout.

"It's lunchtime," he says. "How come you weren't in class this morning?"

"None of your business," I answer.

"Turn in your contest entry yet?" he asks.

"No!" I shout at him. "Why do you think I'm in such a hurry?"

"I dunno," he says. "But I don't think they're due until one."

"One o'clock?" I ask. "How come nobody ever told me that? All they said was Friday!"

"Dunno," says Rollo.

"That's a pretty *M*," says Molly, signing her name.

"What time is it now?" I shout at Rollo.

Rollo looks at his Stanfurd wristwatch. "Half past noon," he says. "Looks like you have half an hour to get it into Scrimshaw's office."

"Phew," I say, relieved. "Just enough time to solve the mystery."

Molly gets off me. I unwrap myself from my banner.

"You haven't solved it yet?" asks Molly.

"No, I haven't it solved it yet. I'm Timmy Failure. That's the whole plan."

"To not solve it?" asks Rollo.

"No, Pop-Tart-head. To solve it. But not *just* solve it. To solve it with *flair*," I explain.

"What does that mean?" asks Molly.

"It means I'm gonna go where all the kids are lining up to turn in their entries and let everyone know that I haven't even *thought* about the mystery."

"What's the point of that?" asks Rollo.

"Because they'll be stunned," I tell him. "Here they've put all this work into the stupid thing and I'm just as casual as can be."

"But you could lose," says Molly.

"Wrong," I answer. "Because while those poor kids are staring at me with their wide eyes, I'll start asking them questions. *Leading* questions. *Professional* questions. 'Did you find the fingerprints on the desk?' 'Did you interview the suspicious janitor?' And those kids will be so intimidated by my technique that they'll answer."

"They will?" asks Molly.

"Of course!" I answer. "And that's when I'll close my eyes, think about what they've told me, and solve the mystery."

"You can do that?" asks Molly.

"I'm Timmy Failure," I remind her. "I can do anything."

"But how will they know you've solved it?" asks Rollo. "You can't shout out the answer to the other contestants."

"Because," I explain to him, "as soon as

I solve it, I'll climb the school's flagpole and hoist my Banner of Greatness."

But Rollo doesn't hear me.

Because the flagpole falls.

"Brakes kaput," says my great-aunt.

CHAPTER 16

The Lying, the Watch, and the Poor Globe

I march down to Principal Scrimshaw's office as a man at the peak of his tactical power.

Like Napoleon in Austerlitz.

← Napoleon

Grant in Vicksburg.

←Grant

Mario in the Mushroom Kingdom.

←Mario

Only to find no mushrooms.

"Where is everybody?" I ask Marilyn, the No-Longer-Smiling Secretary.

"What do you mean?" asks Marilyn.

"The amateurs. They're not lined up. Did they get intimidated like Rollo?"

And as I say his name, I hear his voice.

"Timmy!"

He is lumbering toward me faster than he has ever run the mile in P.E.

"Must you shadow me at every key event in my life?" I ask.

"We have to talk," he says.

"Not now!" I tell him.

"Timmy," says Marilyn. "I don't know what to tell you."

"Tell me about what? I have a contest to enter. Where is everybody?"

"Timmy, my watch!" interrupts Rollo.

"Pipe down, Rollo," I answer.

"They were all here already," says Marilyn.

"The other kids? They came early?"

"Yes. Well, no. They weren't early."

"What are you talking about?" I ask.

She kneels in front of me. Her eyes level to mine.

"Timmy," she says. "It's ten minutes after one."

My left eye twitches. Then my right.

"Mendacity!" I answer. "It was 12:30 five minutes ago."

Rollo holds up his watch.

I peer at Rollo.

"It must have stopped," he says, tapping its face.

I feel the blood rushing to my head. I pivot back to Marilyn.

"This can't be!" I shout. "I'll solve the globe mystery right now!"

"Timmy, I can't," she says. "This is our school's deadline."

"The janitor took the globe! The vice principal took the globe!"

"I can't do it, Timmy," says Marilyn. "I'm sorry."

"It was you! It was Rollo! IT WAS PRINCIPAL SCRIMSHAW'S WIFE!"

At that, I see the blinds open in the office window.

Behind which is Scrimshaw.

"You can change this!" I yell at him.

Scrimshaw points at his watch. Shrugs his shoulders.

"You can change this!" I tell him.

He shakes his head.

"It's just ten stupid minutes!"

"I'm sorry," he mouths.

"Who are you afraid of?" I ask. "The

superintendent? The mayor? I have connections! We'll get them canned!"

But as I pound on the glass, I drop the
Banner of Greatness, the reflection of which
no longer fills the office window.

Allowing me to see deeper into the office.

To the chair in front of Scrimshaw's desk.

And the person in that chair.

Sitting smugly.

"SHENANIGANS!" I scream.

CHAPTER 17

The Entire Universe Has Collapsed

"The deadline was the deadline, Timmy," says my mother. "I'm sure it wasn't Corrina Corrina who made your principal enforce it. She probably had a totally unrelated reason for being in his office. And besides, what good does it do to lock yourself in Uncle Gustav's study?"

"It's not a study," I tell her.

"Then what is it?" she asks.

"A grievance factory," I answer.

Before she can comment, I slide Grievance Card No. 1 under the door.

"What is this?" she asks.

"Read it," I say through the door.

"I had a job interview!" she says. "So I asked your great-aunt to wake you."

"I wouldn't have needed *anyone* to wake

me if someone hadn't fed me sugary cookies just before bed and kept me up half the night."

"So this is all my fault?" she asks.

I slide Grievance Card No. 2 under the door.

"Your great-aunt? Timmy, without her you wouldn't have made it to school at all. You missed the bus. It's not her fault her car broke down."

I slide Grievance Card No. 3 under the door.

"Okay, this is getting absurd," says my mother. "I mean, really, Timmy. Can you act any more ridiculous?"

I shove another card under the door.

"Okay. We're done," says my mother.

"We're not done," I reply.

"Right," she answers. "You haven't given me a card for your great-aunt's bird."

I think about Torpedo Bob. And the things I could probably blame him for.

"I'm not talking about the bird," I answer. "I'm talking about the rotund kid."

"Rollo?" she says. "You're going to blame your best friend?"

"Bingo," I say. "For owning a defective watch. Among a bevy of other faults."

"Wonderful," she says. "Slide me his card."

But I can't.

So I open the door.

"Stack's too big," I say.

CHAPTER 18

Getting a Head

I know that if I am to move forward like the professional that I am, I must first see the past with mature eyes.

And that means acknowledging that others have caused all my problems and blaming them for it.

But I am not yet finished.

I have one more party to blame. For the lies. For the leg. For the slowing me down.

So I travel the necessary distance to do it in person.

And once there, I let him have it.

"CURSE YOU, CARL KOBALINSKI!"

Only now he is headless.
So it feels odd.

CHAPTER 19

Last Train to Glooberville

My journey back from the museum is interrupted by Mr. Eraser Tip.

"I—I—I think I know who swiped Spooney Spoon," stammers Nunzio Benedici.

And I don't have time for it.

"Get ahold of yourself, Benedici," I tell him. "You're talking to a professional."

"I know. Sorry to track you down like this."

"Well, it better be good. I like to use my time on the Buttermobile to think."

"It *is* good," he says. "I think it was Minnie who took it."

"Who's she?"

"It's a he. And he's my cousin."

"What evidence do you have?"

"He just got sent to Glouberman."

"What's Glouberman?"

"Glouberman Academy," he says.

"Don't know it," I say.

"It's the school for—"

"WAIT," I say.

"You know it?" he asks.

"No," I answer. "I just got butter in my eye."

He waits for me to wipe it.

"Go ahead," I say.

"It's the school for bad kids," he continues.

"What'd he do to get sent there?" I ask.

"I dunno. But you have to be bad."

"Bad how, Benedici?"

"I guess acting bad in class and getting bad grades and stuff."

"And what's this Glooberville supposed to do for them?"

"Glouberman," he says. "It's a lot more strict about behavior and all that. Plus, they all get help with their schoolwork. You know, like individual tutors and more time to turn in assignments and—"

"Circumstantial!" I shout as I pull on the rope for Total to stop.

"What's that mean?" he asks.

"It means put more butter on my head," I say, handing him a cube. "I have somewhere I have to be."

"I can't," he says.

"Why?" I sneer. "You too important to help a hard-nosed detective navigate the gritty streets of an unforgiving city?"

"No," he says. "I'm lactose intolerant."

CHAPTER 20
'Cause He's a Voodoo Child

Back in school, I listen to Rollo Tookus tell me what "lactose intolerant" means.

"It means an inability to digest dairy products," he says.

"Are you sure?" I ask. "Because it sounded like something anti-detective."

"I'm sure," he says. "And will you put that thing away? It looks nothing like me."

The "thing" he's referring to is my new
Rollo Tookus voodoo doll.

ROLLO TOOKUS
VOODOO DOLL

"You sabotaged the most important day of
my life," I say, holding up the doll. "And this
is the emotional support I need."

I poke the doll in the eye with my finger.

"Feel anything?" I ask.

"No," he says.

"Give me that!" booms a voice from behind.

It is Mr. Purgatoni. Our geography teacher.
And he is holding the doll by its head.

"I have you kids in my class for one hour a week to teach you geography," he says, shaking the doll violently as he points.

"Do you feel *that*?" I ask Rollo.

Purgatoni clears his throat. "And the least you can do is pay attention."

It's true.

The school is trying a new experiment where we get to leave our regular classroom a few times a week to learn certain subjects from different teachers.

Mondays are English with Ms. Kelmsley.

Wednesdays are science with Mr. Peters.

And Fridays are geography with the guy now holding the voodoo Rollo.

I'm not sure why they picked Mr. Purgatoni to teach geography. Especially since he normally teaches wood shop. Maybe it's because he only teaches half a day and has his afternoons free.

Or maybe it's because he's the most boring person they could find.

"I would gladly pay attention if your lecture style were more gripping," I explain to Mr. Purgatoni. "As it is, I find it rather jejune."

Rollo pulls away from me.

"Jejune?" he says. "You think I'm dull?"

"Dull," I respond. "Pedestrian. But don't be discouraged. You seem like a nice man."

A hush comes over the class. Even Molly Moskins sits stone-faced.

← Stone-faced Molly Moskins

"This is a referral to the principal's office," says Mr. Purgatoni, ripping a pink sheet from a pad. The sudden nature of the gesture causes the voodoo doll to drop from his other hand and land headfirst on the classroom's hard floor.

I look over at Rollo.

"Surely you felt that."

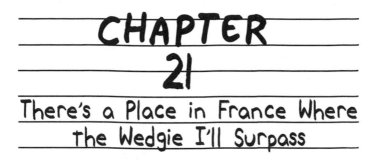

CHAPTER 21

There's a Place in France Where the Wedgie I'll Surpass

The solarium is sweltering.

The mood is menacing.

And we are beset by Bingo's leaf blower.

"Will you please turn that thing off?" I yell at Bingo, my great-aunt's gardener. "I'm in the middle of a motivational speech."

But he doesn't hear me.

So I climb back on my chair and continue my inspirational speech to Total. Only this time louder.

"'YOU ASK, WHAT IS OUR POLICY? IT IS TO WAGE WAR AGAINST A MONSTROUS

TYRANNY, NEVER SURPASSED IN THE DARK LAMENTABLE CATALOGUE OF HUMAN CRIME!'"

Total rolls on his back to scratch his rear end.

Scratch
Scratch

"'WE SHALL NOT FLAG OR FAIL! WE SHALL GO ON TO THE END!'"

The blower suddenly stops. And I am left shouting at top volume.

"'AND WE SHALL FIGHT IN FRANCE!'"

My great-aunt rolls in on her Boom Boom Shoewheels.

"You're fighting in France?" she asks.

"Is there no privacy in this place?" I moan.

"Because if you're fighting in France, I should go with you."

I get off my chair.

"It's from a book of speeches by Winston Churchill," I tell her. "I found it when I locked myself in the study."

"You locked yourself in the study?" she asks.

"It's like he *knew* the Wedgie," I say.

"Well, if you're fighting the Wedgie, I'm fighting the Wedgie," she says.

She pauses to scratch her hip.

"Who's the Wedgie?" she asks.

"Never mind," I answer. "And I don't need your help."

"It's always good to have allies," she says.

"For your information, I have a fifteen-hundred-pound ally on my side. He is a predator. He is feared. And he is at the top of the Arctic food chain."

But as I say this, I hear a high-pitched
squeal.

And see a certain ally running.

And turn back to my great-aunt.

"When can you start?"

CHAPTER 22

A River Named Bob

I am failing geography.

Presumably for answers such as this:

Name the longest river in the world.

Probably already has a
name. But fine, I'll
call it Bob.

Ditto my English class, where Ms. Kelmsley did not approve of my book report on *The Lion, the Witch, and the Wardrobe:*

BOOK REPORT

I'm guessing the lion ate the witch's clothes.

My math class is not going much better.

A man is traveling 65 mph on a train from Cleveland to Pittsburgh, a distance of 130 miles. The train left Cleveland at 9:00 pm. The man wants to know what time he'll arrive in Pittsburgh. What would you tell him?

That he should ask the conductor.

"I don't understand what's happening," says Mr. Jenkins, who has kept me after class. "You haven't had these problems since Mr. Crocus taught this class."

Ah, Old Man Crocus. A teacher so ill-prepared for my greatness that he had to move to an island to escape it.

"Is it because of what happened with the detective contest?" asks Mr. Jenkins.

"The detective contest?" I ask.

"The missing globe one," he says.

"Oh, that?" I say. "No, no, no, no, no."

"But I heard you were upset about how you lost."

"Lost? I didn't *lose,* Mr. Jenkins. They don't announce the winner for a number of weeks."

"Well, maybe 'lost' isn't the word. I just mean how they wouldn't accept your entry."

"Ah, yes," I say. "You're referring to The Great Injustice."

"Okay," he says.

I crack my knuckles.

"Well, Mr. Jenkins, you'll learn after you live enough years on this planet that the world is just *filled* with injustice. We detectives see it more than you civilians."

"Is that so?" he asks.

"It is, Mr. Jenkins. Shenanigans abound."

"Well, I don't know if that's true, but I'm glad to hear you're not angry."

"The world's great detectives don't *get* angry, sir. They get—"

I stop myself.

"They get what, Timmy?"

"They get better grades, Mr. Jenkins. They make every effort to get—"

WHAM!

I am hit on the head by a flying envelope.

"Get down! Get down!" I scream at Jenkins. "We're under attack."

I dive on his head to protect him. We both fall to the floor.

"Must have come through that window!" I shout.

"Please get off my head," says Mr. Jenkins.

"Remain calm," I tell him.

I get off his head.

And kneel beside the offending envelope, the topside of which is blank.

Careful to not contaminate it with my own

fingerprints, I use the end of my detective-grade scarf to flip it over.

And there, on the reverse side, find some very disturbing markings.

CHAPTER
23
The Tell-Tale Hearts

"It's obviously the work of an assassin," I tell my great-aunt. "But who?"

She is examining the envelope. The one with the hearts on it.

"Was there anything inside?" she asks.

"Of course," I say. "Have my secretary pull the letter from the filing cabinet."

But he can't.

Because his head is stuck in a cereal box.

I grab the letter myself and hand it to my great-aunt.

She glances at it.

"Timmy, this isn't the work of an assassin," she says.

"Are you kidding?" I ask. "Look at it."

"I *am* looking at it," she says. "I think it's somebody who likes you."

I bang my forehead against the solarium glass.

"You see now why I don't like to hire amateurs?" I ask my great-aunt. "I should have known better. You can't even get air-conditioning installed in this sweltering house!"

"You're standing in the solarium," she replies. "It's *supposed* to be warm!"

"I have a polar bear!" I remind her.

"All right, fine, Timmy. Maybe the heat is getting to all of us. What do *you* think the letter means?"

"It's *code*. Don't you see?"

"All I see is a bunch of hearts."

"Think," I tell her. "The heart is what keeps you alive. This person is threatening that."

"They want you—*kaput*?"

"Of course! Why do you think they threw it through the window? This envelope has sharp corners. Who knows what damage it could have done?"

"I suppose."

"And they knew Jenkins was in there. So they didn't care if they took *him* out in the process."

"Oh, my," she says. "What do we do?"

"We give me time to think."

"I can do that," she says, steadying herself against my shoulder and rolling toward the door.

"Where are you going?" I ask.

"Giving you time to think," she says. "Besides, I have a board meeting to get to."

"Whoa, whoa, whoa," I say. "You're hardly on our board."

"Not *your* board, Timmy. It's for something called an entrepreneurs' fund."

"Entrepreneurs' fund? What's an entrepreneurs' fund?"

"I don't know, exactly. I think they give money to business-type folk. I'm on all sorts of boards. Charities, schools, museums, hospitals. I guess they figure that's all an old woman like me is good for. To sit there and hear boring people give long speeches."

"Hmmph," I answer. "It's hard for me to relate to the lives of boring people."

"Me too," she says.

And as she says it, she stares down at her Boom Boom Shoewheels.

I stare at them also.

And then look back up at her.

"One day you'll sell a million of those!" I blurt out.

She smiles.

"And we'll fight 'em in France!" she yells back.

CHAPTER
24
It's a Long, Long Way to Topiary

I'm watching Bingo make an elephant out of a bush.

"Why do you do that?" I ask.

"Your great-aunt likes it," he says. "She says it adds a little fun to an otherwise dull neighborhood. I like it, too. Though I'd like it a lot more if she'd pay me."

"She doesn't pay you?"

"Oh, I shouldn't say that. She eventually does. Most of the time. But it's okay. The truth is she's such a nice woman that I'd probably do it for free."

"Can I climb up there?" I ask.

"Okay," he says, "but be careful."

I climb up the ladder and sit on the elephant's back, high enough to see into the surrounding yards.

"She's right," I tell him. "Nothing but old, boring people."

"Except for the place next door," he says, pointing to a swing set. "They must have some young kids."

I stand on the elephant's back and try to find them.

"HULLOOOOOOO!" I yell.

Which startles Bingo.

Who lops off the elephant's leg.

"Please don't yell like that," he says, staring at the damaged elephant.

"Can you make a polar bear?" I ask.

But before he can answer, I hear a loud cry.

"TIMMY!"

It's my mother.

And her shout startles Bingo.

Who lops off the elephant's tail.

"Nooooo!" cries Bingo.

"Get down before you break your neck, Timmy! I want to talk to you!"

I climb down the ladder.

"Why is your principal calling me for a meeting at his office?"

I shrug my shoulders.

"Why, Timmy?" she shouts.

"Could you people *please* stop yelling?" asks a desperate Bingo, holding the elephant's tail.

Elephant's
Tail

"Why, Timmy?" she says in a softer voice.

"I dunno," I answer.

"Timmy, I don't understand. I thought all these problems with your grades and every-thing were behind us. You were doing so well."

I shrug my shoulders again.

"What is it? Is it the contest? Are you still upset about the contest?"

"No," I say.

"I want you to be very honest, Timmy," she says. "Is it me? Is it about my losing my job? Losing the apartment? Not finding work? Having to move all the time?"

I think about that.

"It's all this change, isn't it?" she asks. "You don't like change. Nobody does. You can tell me, Timmy. Is that what it is? There's no shame in admitting that. Is that what's going on?"

I think about what she's saying. And look into her eyes.

"BINGO!" I answer.

And I hear a loud snip.

"ARRGGHHH!" cries the gardener.

CHAPTER
25
Stumping the Detective

"It's my head," I say to Rollo Tookus, holding up a tree stump.

"Looks like a tree stump," says Rollo.

"You look like a tree stump," I answer. "It's an extraordinary likeness."

"Who did it for you?"

"My great-aunt's gardener. He does tapioca sculptures."

"Topiary," says Rollo. "Tapioca is a pudding."

"You know nothing about art," I tell him. "I suggest you stay out of this."

"You're the one who brought it to show-and-tell," says Rollo.

"Do I have to separate you two?" asks Mr. Jenkins from the front of the class.

"Now look what you've done," whispers Rollo to me.

"Now look what *you've* done," I answer back.

"It was me, Mr. Jenkins!" says Molly Moskins, rising to her feet. "I was the one who was talking!"

"Sit down, Molly," says Mr. Jenkins.

"What are you doing?" I whisper to Molly Moskins.

"You keep getting in trouble," she says. "So I'm saving you."

"Class, if I could have your attention for a moment," says Mr. Jenkins.

Molly winks at me.

"I don't normally do this," continues Mr. Jenkins, "but I just wanted to congratulate a person in this class for receiving the only perfect score I've given on a math test this semester."

Rollo's head begins to bob back and forth like a maraca in a salsa band.

It is something that happens before any test or at the mere mention of grades.

"And the person I want to congratulate is Corrina Corrina," says Mr. Jenkins.

"Noooo!" shouts Rollo Tookus, his head accelerating even more. "We're probably graded on a curve! I could end up with a B plus! And a B plus is the worst thing in the world!"

"Calm down, Rollo," says Mr. Jenkins. "You got an A as well."

Rollo takes a deep breath. His head slows down.

"But Corrina Corrina was truly exceptional," says Mr. Jenkins. "And I wanted to give her some recognition."

"And I would like some recognition, too!" I announce from atop my desk. "Why, just look at my beautiful sculpture."

"What are you doing?" asks Rollo.

"None of your business," I answer.

"Timmy, get off your desk," says Mr. Jenkins.

"Timmy, you'll get in trouble!" cries Molly

Moskins, tugging on my arm.

"What weird, secretive thing are you up to now?" asks Rollo.

"You're the weirdo!" I shout at Rollo.

"Are you going to get down from there or not?" asks Mr. Jenkins.

"Okay, okay," I answer. And I begin to climb down.

But don't quite make it.

Because I am tackled by an overprotective Molly Moskins.

Causing me, my desk, and my binder to crash to the ground.

Where my binder pops open.

And a document goes flying.

And the secret is out.

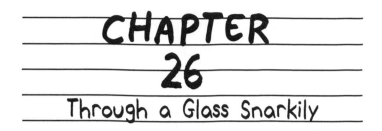

CHAPTER
26
Through a Glass Snarkily

"You're trying to get kicked out of school!" shouts Rollo Tookus to me in the boys' bathroom.

"Keep your voice down," I say as I check under the stalls for feet.

"It's all right here," he says, holding the document that flew out of my binder.

"ARE YOU A GREAT DETECTIVE?"
School Submission Deadlines

Carverette Elementary
March 7

Stonewall Elementary
March 5

Valentino Elementary
March 7

Reebler Elementary
March 5

Glouberman Academy
April 2

Williams Charter School
March 5

"I know nothing," I blurt out.

"You found out that Glouberman Academy's contest deadline is one month later than every other school's. So you decided to behave so badly that you get sent there. Then you could enter the contest after all!"

"Mendacity!" I reply.

Nunzio Benedici pushes open the door.

"OUT!" I yell, setting down my tree stump to block the door.

"It's the truth, Timmy! And it's idiotic!" bellows Rollo.

"Keep your voice down!" I answer.

The door opens again, knocking over my tree stump. "I love you, Timmy Failure!" cries Molly Moskins.

"Get out of the boys' room!" grumbles Rollo, nudging her outside.

"Timmy's my hero!" she cheers from behind the closed door.

"It's just a contest, Timmy," says Rollo, with his back pressed against the door to keep Molly out. "A stupid contest."

"It's a contest that will set me up for the rest of my life!" I snap back.

The door opens again. "I really need to go to the bathroom," says Nunzio.

"OUT!" I cry.

"Timmy, five hundred dollars does not set you up for the rest of your life," says Rollo.

"You know *nothing*," I say through gritted teeth. "*Nothing* about detective work. *Nothing* about the real world."

"Maybe," he says. "But I know your plan is stupid. And shortsighted. And even if it weren't, you don't get kicked out and sent to Glouberman just for getting bad grades and being obnoxious. Those kids are *bad,* Timmy. Very bad."

"Get out of my way, Rollo," I tell him, picking up my tree stump. "You're the reason I missed that stupid deadline."

He steps away from the door.

And as he does, it bursts open.

And he is pummeled by a flying Molly.
And a flying Nunzio.

And a shower of eraser tips.

And from the bottom of that collapsed universe, Rollo cannot stop me.

Cannot stop me as I walk down the long hall with Tree Stump Timmy.

Cannot stop me as I walk toward the office of Alexander Scrimshaw.

Cannot stop me when, just outside Scrimshaw's window, I hoist the stump high above my head.

"THIS IS TAPIOCA ME!" I yell, waving the tree stump back and forth. "TIMMY FAILURE! A MAN WHO IS NOBODY'S FOOL! NOT THE WEDGIE'S! NOT THIS SCHOOL'S! AND NOT *YOURS,* SCRIMSHAW, YOU DEADLINE-FIXING, SHENANIGAN-LOVING PURVEYOR OF MONSTROUS—"

The blinds rise.

"—tyrannies," I finish.

As I see Scrimshaw.

And behind him in his office a second person.

Who I call Mom.

Whose appointment with Scrimshaw so slipped my mind that I am stunned and lose my balance.

And accidentally fall.

Tapioca Me–first.

Through Scrimshaw's window.

"Okay, now you're kicked out," says Rollo.

CHAPTER
27
Attack of the Gloubermans

Glouberman Academy has a lot of big kids.

I am not one of them.

And that can be bad. Because word is that kids here get flattened.

And flown.

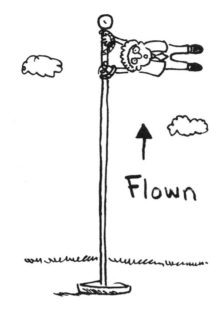

Flown

And crammed into juice boxes.

Crammed
into
juice
boxes

JUICE

But not me.

Because I have connections.

Like Minnie the Magnificent.

Minnie
the
Magnificent

Minnie is Nunzio Benedici's cousin. And Nunzio is a client.

As a result, Minnie knows who I am. Knows my reputation. And knows that I am partners with a fierce Arctic predator.

Fierce Arctic predator

As such, Minnie has tremendous respect for me. (And I, in turn, have respect for him, as shown by my giving him my lunch money every day and adding the words *the Magnificent* to the end of his name.)

This relationship has a number of advantages. For one thing, I'm losing weight. For another thing, I have time to focus on the biggest case of my life.

A case that is no longer about a missing globe. But is now about defeating injustice. And overcoming shenanigans. And obliterating the Worldwide Enemy of Da Goodness In Everything.

Which I will do.

Despite another threat on my being.

This one appeared mysteriously in my backpack.

And that was no mistake.

Because whoever did it needed to show that (1) they can still reach my person and (2) they still want me gone.

That was made even clearer by the note inside.

It doesn't take a genius to figure out what that means. Just add a couple of letters.

As in "I just missed maiming you with that last envelope."

But this time, the suspect left a vital clue.

A sticky note at the bottom of the letter.

Which can only mean one thing:

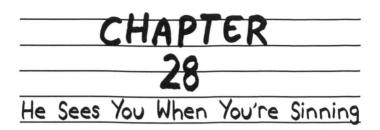

CHAPTER
28
He Sees You When You're Sinning

My mother has a long history of reacting poorly to minor incidents.

Like when I sawed through the support beams in our attic.

MY OFFICE NEEDED MORE HEADROOM.

And sledgehammered a hole in my bed-room wall.

But she has not said a word since the day I broke Scrimshaw's window.

Maybe she blames herself for suddenly appearing in the window and startling me.

Or maybe she blames Scrimshaw.

Or maybe she realizes it's all the fault of the Wedgie.

Whatever it is, it works for me. Because if there's one thing a detective doesn't need, it's distractions on the home front.

Particularly when he's writing his theme song.

"I like it," says my great-aunt.

"So does my Arctic business partner," I answer. "It's a compelling piece."

I play the song again.

"I particularly like how you only play one note," she says.

"Yes," I say. "It's what's known as minimalism."

My great-aunt smiles and sits beside me on the piano bench.

"Timmy, at the risk of appearing very un-detective-like, I just want to say that if you ever want to talk about things, I'm a darn good listener."

"What is there to talk about?" I say.

"I don't know," she says. "Life."

"Life?" I smirk, staring at her.

"I told you," she said. "Not very detective-like."

"Yeah, well, right now I spend every hour I have outside of the prison known as Glouberman Academy either working on the biggest case of my era or writing my theme song. So I'm not quite sure I have much 'life' to discuss."

"Right, right," she says. "I guess I just meant how you felt about everything."

"I feel fine," I tell her.

"Of course," she says. "I should have known that. Detectives are much better equipped to deal with life than normal people."

"*Civilians,* we call them."

"Yes, civilians," she says. "Like me. We civilians can have a tough go of it sometimes."

I look around her large parlor.

"Hmmph," I say. "It doesn't look like it."

"Why?" she asks. "'Cause I live in a big house?"

"A big, expensive house," I answer. "You should see some of the grim realities faced by a crime investigator on the streets."

"Oh, I imagine," she says.

"It's not pretty," I add.

She stares blankly at my sheet music but says nothing.

I look away toward the drapes.

"You okay?" she asks.

I hesitate and then swing back around to face her.

"And if *you* ever want to talk, you can probably talk to me," I blurt out.

She smiles and puts her arm around my shoulder.

"Though I would prefer it be about agency business," I add, pointing my finger at her.

She looks again at the sheet music and sings.

"GREAT TIM-MY SEES ALL OF YOUR SINS, SO DO NOT TRY SHEEE-NAN-I-GANS!"

Causing my Arctic business partner to do

the one thing he always does whenever someone sings.

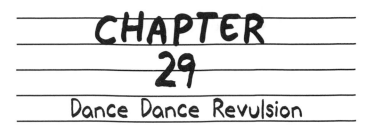

CHAPTER
29
Dance Dance Revulsion

"School's not the same without you," says Rollo Tookus.

"I imagine there's great sadness," I say from atop my wounded elephant.

"I don't know about that," says Rollo. "But Molly Moskins sure misses you."

"Well, I don't miss her," I answer. "The girl has no sense of personal space."

"She wanted to come visit you also, but she doesn't know where you live and I didn't think you wanted me to tell her."

"Of course I don't. Who needs that distraction? I have one week to solve the biggest case of the millennium."

"Is that why you're sitting on a bush?" asks Rollo.

"It's an elephant. And it's where I do my best thinking."

"Oh, that reminds me," says Rollo, pulling a piece of paper out of his backpack. "Did you ever get one of these? The school handed them out a while back. It's a list of possible suspects for the globe case. I thought I'd bring you one in case you didn't have it."

> **Superintendent Dobbs has narrowed down the list of possible suspects.**
>
> **They are:**
>
> **Ms. Mabley — Reebler**
> **Mr. Purgatoni — Carverette**
> **Mr. Ryan — Valentino**
> **Ms. Kelmsley — Carverette**
> **Mr. Traynor — Stonewall**
> **Mr. Roberts — Glouberman**
> **Ms. Swann — Williams**

"Well, this is worthless," I say.

"What do you mean?"

"What do I *mean*?" I answer, pulling my hair in frustration. "You don't recognize a ruse when you see it?"

"Timmy, I don't think the school district would purposely misdirect you by—"

"Of course they would!" I reply. "Have you learned nothing from recent events? Please don't waste my time with this."

I hand him back the list.

"Fine," Rollo replies. "Figure out your own suspects. And see how wrong you turn out to be when you come to the dance."

"Dance?" I ask. "What dance?"

"Don't they tell you anything at Glouberman? They're announcing the winner of the detective contest at an all-schools dance."

"A dance! Who likes dances?"

I spot my business partner out of the corner of my eye.

"Do some work!" I snap at Total.

"And you have to bring a date," says Rollo.

"A DATE!" I yell from atop my tapioca elephant. "Can this *get* any more farcical?"

My cry is so loud that it disturbs the old man in the yard next door.

"Mind keeping it down?" asks the man. "I'm reading to my grandchild."

I get off the elephant. And point at Rollo.

"Timmy Failure does *not* go to school dances. And he does *not* bring dates. And he does *not* dance."

"Well, that's too bad," says Rollo. "Because

I figured that with the detective contest and all, you'd be going for sure. And I maybe sort of said something I shouldn't have."

"What?" I ask.

"Nothing," he says.

"WHAT?" I ask again.

"Well, a certain girl sort of thought that, well, you'd be asking her to the dance. And I sort of told her that, well, you probably would."

I stare at my round friend with a mixture of revulsion and horror.

"You didn't."

"I might have," he mutters.

I feel my head about to explode.

"And this certain girl might have already gone out and, uh, bought herself a, well, brand-new dress, just for the occasion."

"ARRRRRRGHHHHHHHH!" I yell with enough fury to be heard by the old man next door.

And the rest of the block.

And the rest of the city.

A city that contains one little girl who was no doubt staring into the mirror at that very moment.

CHAPTER 30

See You Spoon

It is high noon at the Glouberman dining facility.

And the elephants are feeding at the trough.

Including one elephant whose lunch I sub-
sidized myself.

Minnie the Magnificent. Cousin of Nunzio.
Recipient of my lunch money.

I watch as he dips his spoon into his soup.
And swallows a spoonful.

And dips in his spoon. And swallows a
spoonful.

And dips in his spoon.

And it is then that I see what is on the end
of that spoon.

A dog's head.

And as he finishes his first bowl of soup and begins a second, my detective instinct takes over.

And I realize what I am seeing.

And rush to make a note in my detective log.

There is a sculpture called *The Thinker*.

It looks like this:

← The Thinker

I am now imitating it from atop my great-aunt's fountain.

I am imitating it because I have only a few days left to think about the Biggest Case of the Millennium.

Something I used to do from atop the quiet sanctity of my tapioca elephant. Until Rollo and the old man next door ruined it with their incessant chatter.

My great-aunt's fountain is also convenient for my business partner. For him, the water is both a cool respite from the hot solarium and a shelter to hide his large body from his dive-bombing nemesis.

Well, *most* of his large body.

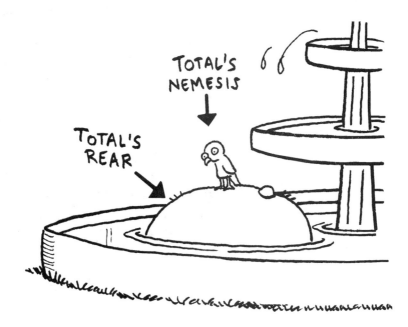

TOTAL'S NEMESIS

TOTAL'S REAR

Which is more than I can hide of my body
when I am stunned by an unwanted intruder.

"You're *The Thinker*!" trills Molly Moskins.

"What are you doing here?" I shout.

"I'm visiting my date!"

"I'm not your date, Molly Moskins. I'm not going to the dance! And how'd you even *find* this place?"

"I have my ways," she says, winking. "And you are, too, going! That's when they reveal you're the big winner!"

"For your information, Molly Moskins, I am currently making arrangements to appear *in absentia*. That means I'll be there in spirit, but not in body."

She smiles. Oblivious to my words.

"The theme is A Romantic Night in Paris," she chirps. "Paris, Timmy! Do you know where that is?"

I do, but I don't answer.

"*I* know where it is, Timmy! It's in France! The most romantic place in the universe! Should we practice our slow dances now?"

But I don't answer.

Because from atop my thinking fountain, I am once again *The Thinker*.

Thinking harder than I ever have before.

About what is going to have to happen next for me to win the contest.

So I climb down off my fountain. And walk toward Molly.

And take both of her hands.

And say the only thing I can.

"Molly Moskins, you're under arrest."

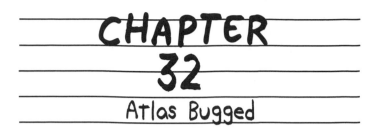

CHAPTER
32
Atlas Bugged

"You can't arrest Molly Moskins!" cries Rollo Tookus.

"What are you doing calling me on the Timmyline?" I answer. "It's for paying clients only."

"I'm calling because you've arrested an innocent person!" he says.

"Relax," I answer. "The perpetrator has been released on her own recognizance. That means she's free until trial. It was a very generous move on my part."

"Generous? Timmy, she did nothing wrong!" says Rollo.

I contemplate hanging up.

"You're really testing my patience, Rollo Tookus. But I'll try to make this simple. Molly Moskins is a criminal mastermind. A mastermind who stole the superintendent's globe. And if you think otherwise, then you—like many other amateurs—have been fooled by her duplicitous ways."

"That's ridiculous."

"You're ridiculous. *I'm* about to win a massive amount of money. And establish my agency as an international conglomerate. And make the whole world mine."

"Yeah, well, before you do all that, you need to know that the schools have provided clues to the contestants. I was going to give them to you, but I figured you'd ignore them just like you ignored the suspect list."

"La-la-la, I cannot hear you, la-la-la."

"Listen, Timmy!" shouts Rollo. "If you're going to go off and accuse Molly Moskins, you need to *hear* some of these clues. Like the fact that the globe was stolen between two and three o'clock in the afternoon. *When Molly was in class.* And the fact that it was bolted down with some special screwdriver. Which I *guarantee* you Molly doesn't have."

"La-la-la-la-la, amateur, amateur, amateur, la-la-la-la-la-la—"

"TIMMY FAILURE, YOU EITHER LISTEN TO ME OR YOU LOSE THIS CONTEST!" snaps Rollo.

I stop la-la-la-ing.

"I'm hanging up now, Rollo."

"Timmy, don't."

"I am."

"Timmy, please. I'm just trying to help."

"Perhaps. But you've crossed a professional line. And you know nothing."

"Then tell me."

"Fine, Rollo. I'll tell you one thing. One thing you must swear an oath on your ever-loving GPA to never share with anyone else."

"I swear," says Rollo.

"And if you break the oath, you will not graduate with a 4.6 GPA."

"Okay," he says.

"And you will not go to Stanfurd."

"Okay," he says.

"And you will be forced to pick up trash by the highway for the rest of your life."

"I swear! I swear, already!" he cries.

I lower my voice and continue.

"When you came to my great-aunt's house a few days ago, you said that Molly didn't know where I lived."

"Yeah," he says. "So?"

"So then she found my house and told me the theme of the dance. Which was about Paris. Which is in France."

"So?" he asks. "What's your point?"

"My point?" I answer. "My point is that you're an amateur! Do I have to draw you a picture?"

"Yeah, Timmy, I guess you do. And then maybe you should e-mail it to me, so I can be enlightened just like you."

So I ignore the snooty sarcasm and draw him a picture.

A picture of the only way Molly Moskins could suddenly have found my great-aunt's house.

And Paris, France.

That being a map.

A big, round map.
Or as some might call it . . .
A stolen globe.

And suddenly.
The whole world is mine.

CHAPTER 33

C'mon, Minnie, Light My Fire

I've had a slight bump in my professional relationship with Minnie the Magnificent. And that has resulted in a minor inconvenience.

That being that I am standing in my Mr. Froggie underwear.

Now, having your clothes taken by the largest kid at Glouberman Academy is one thing. But having it done on the day you have to explain *Bridge to Terabithia* to the rest of the class is another.

I have warned my mother many times about buying me Mr. Froggie underwear, and now the day of reckoning has come.

Fortunately, I was able to borrow a shirt from the Lost and Found office. Unfortunately, it had Hello Catty on it.

But I could not find any pants.

So I was forced to use the book itself to cover Mr. Froggie.

But that's what happens in a professional relationship when you do not hold up your end of the bargain. And hold it up I did not.

For when my mother sent me to school today, she failed to provide me with lunch money. And that meant that Minnie the Magnificent did not have lunch money.

And that meant that someone had a rumbly in his tumbly.

And that meant that someone would be staying after class.

But that is life at Glouberman Academy. And that is okay.

Because I know now that I have solved the Biggest Case of the Millennium. And that my agency is on the verge of going global. And that the brilliance of the Timmy name will soon be known on all nine continents.

So until then, I need only enjoy the camaraderie of my sometimes overzealous classmates. As I did today. When together we delighted in a spirited bonfire.

Made only slightly less delightful by Minnie's comments.

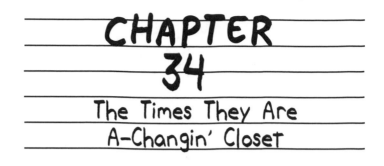

CHAPTER 34

The Times They Are A-Changin' Closet

I am shopping for a new scarf with my business partner.

And am having trouble finding just the right size.

TOO BIG?

My business partner has an abysmal sense of fashion. But I bring him anyway. Mostly because he needs a break from Torpedo Bob.

And the shopping has been productive. Because while looking for the scarf, I have found a majestic robe. One that the store will embroider with any message I want.

Which I have had them do.

Only to find that they are poor spellers.

But they offer it to me at half price. So I try it on in the dressing room.

And am disturbed by an all too familiar voice.

"You in there, Timmy?"

It is Rollo Tookus. The blight that haunts my harvest.

"Sorry to interrupt," he says from behind the dressing-room door. "But your mom said I could find you here. And I need to talk to you about the detective contest."

I swing open the door and yank him into the dressing room.

"Are you insane?" I ask. "Talking about

a critically sensitive topic like that in the middle of a public hallway?"

"Sorry," he says, looking at my clothes. "Hey, nice bathrobe."

"What do you want, Rollo? And make it quick. Your wide girth is not suited to this tight space."

"I know the solution to the contest," he says.

"Not this again!" I tell him. "I told you. I've already solved it!"

"No, no, no," he says. "You were right about all that."

"Of course I was right."

"Yeah," says Rollo. "I thought about it more, and the fact that Molly could find your house definitely means she stole the globe."

"We're crammed in here like sweat socks in a suitcase so you can tell me THAT?" I shout.

"That's not it!" yells Rollo.

"Everything okay in there?" asks a female voice. "I hear yelling."

I see the saleswoman's bright-red shoes below the door of the dressing room.

"No!" I tell her. "I need slippers to go with my robe! And please, spend as much time as you need to find just the right pair!"

"Uh, all right," she answers, walking off.

"There," I say to Rollo. "I've bought us some time. Now, hurry up before we're thrown out for exceeding the spatial limits of this dressing room."

"Fine," says Rollo. "I'll make this quick. You're going to lose the contest."

I suddenly wish I had the slippers now. So I could pummel the round head of Rollo Tookus.

"What in the name of Stanfurd University and all things you hold sacred are you talking about *now*?" I ask.

"Shenanigans," he says.

"Shenanigans?" I ask.

"Shenanigans," he repeats. "Just like you feared."

I grit my teeth.

"Start talking, Rollo Tookus."

"Well, you have the right answer to the contest. It's Molly Moskins. But it's not the answer they're looking for."

"What are you talking about?" I ask him. "What's the answer they're looking for?"

"Mr. Purgatoni."

"Purgatoni!" I cry. "That's absurd."

"Right. It's absurd. But here's what they're going to say," Rollo explains, wiping the sweat from his forehead.

"Purgatoni and the other teachers from our school have monthly meetings with the superintendent. That's where they'll say Purgatoni first saw the globe."

"Fine," I tell him. "So did every other teacher!"

"Right. But they're gonna say that Purgatoni had a motive. And the motive was that he got assigned to teach geography. And he needed a globe to learn the subject."

I see red shoes below the door again.

"I forgot to ask what size you are," says the saleswoman.

"Use your judgment!" I shout. "And please, no more questions!"

I hear the woman stomp off.

"Keep going," I tell Rollo. "I want to hear this nonsense."

"Well, then there's the window of opportunity in which to commit the crime. All the other teachers are busy teaching between two and three o'clock. But not Purgatoni. He has his afternoons free."

"Oh, what amateurs!" I cry.

"They sure are," says Rollo. "But that's not even the stupidest part. The stupidest part is the clincher they'll be relying on."

"What clincher?" I ask.

"The fact that Purgatoni also teaches wood shop. They'll say that that's how he had the means to pull this off. He's the only person who would have had the special screwdriver."

"Mendacity!" I shout. "The real perpetrator is Molly Moskins!"

"Of course," says Rollo. "It's all mendacity. But that's not what this contest is about. You said it yourself. The fix is in."

I grab Rollo by the nonexistent lapels of his Stanfurd shirt.

"How do you KNOW all this?" I plead.

He looks from side to side.

"Have you forgotten who my tutor is?"

Of course.

The biggest fly in the ointment of my friendship with Rollo Tookus.

His tutor.

HIS TUTOR
(Face once again blurred to protect your retinas.)

The Wedgie. As unprofessional and incompetent as ever. Unable to keep her mouth shut.

A low-rent detective whose loose lips will now sink her amateurish ships.

Because now I know.

The scheme.

The ruse.

The shenanigans.

So I will ignore the answer I know to be correct. And turn in the absurd one. And beat them at their own game.

I let go of my best friend's shirt and grab him by his large head.

"Rollo Tookus, your round, sweaty head contains the finest amateur detective mind in this town. Perhaps the nation. You should be very proud."

"Thank you, Timmy," says Rollo. As he is smacked on the head by a pair of flying slippers.

I pick up the slippers.

"Nope," I say. "Definitely not the right size."

CHAPTER 35

Snarl at Carl

On the day before I turn in my contest entry and establish my credentials as the Smartest Person in the World, I have a few choice words for the pretender to the title.

Headless though he may be.

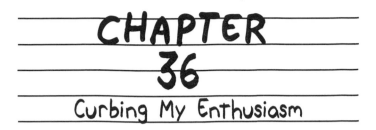

CHAPTER
36
Curbing My Enthusiasm

I do not believe in omens.

But if I did, waking up to an empty cage, some scattered feathers, and a fat-cheeked polar bear would not be a good one.

Furious, I run to Gustav's old closet and grab one of his ties.

And muzzle the bear.

"That does it!" I yell at him. "That does it! I can't take it anymore! I try to be patient with you! And *this* is how you reward me? *This* is your thanks?"

Total lies down on his back. Hoping I'll scratch his stomach.

"You've jeopardized everything. *Everything,*" I tell him. "We'll be kicked out of the house. We'll have nowhere to live. What were you *thinking*?"

But the fact is that I know what he was thinking. He hated Torpedo Bob. He dreaded him. So he acted out. Reverted to his Arctic instincts.

But that's not okay when you're a detective. Detectives keep their head.

"There will be consequences for this," I tell my business partner. "Big, fat, serious consequences."

But not now. Now I have to deal with the crisis at hand. Flush the evidence. Fabricate a story. Fool the mother.

So I gather the feathers. Run to the bathroom. Flush them down the toilet.

And get ready for school as though nothing has happened.

Comb my hair. Brush my teeth.

And hear my mother yell.

"Timmy, where are you?"

My left eye twitches. Then my right.

"I KNOW NOTHING!" I yell back.

"What?" she asks, walking into the bathroom.

I glance at the water in the toilet bowl. And see a feather that didn't flush.

I slam down the toilet seat. And jump on the toilet.

"What are you doing, Timmy?"

"Morning calisthenics," I say. "I hop on the toilet. Then I flush it," I say, flushing the toilet and hoping the last feather disappears.

"Well, don't," she says. "You're wasting water. Why do you do stuff like that?"

She leans back against the bathroom counter and crosses her arms.

I say nothing.

"Timmy, we need to talk."

"I've told you, I know nothing."

"About what?"

"Nothing. I know nothing about nothing."

"Please just be normal for a second," she says, pointing at me. "And get down off the toilet."

I step down to the floor.

"First off, I don't want you to worry. Because what I'm about to tell you is my problem. Not yours."

My hopes soar. She is going to blame herself for the bird.

"In fact, from your point of view, this is probably great news."

Well, that's an exaggeration. I mean, I certainly didn't like Torpedo Bob. But I'm hardly going to celebrate his passing.

"Well, Timmy, I'll just say it," she says. "You no longer have to go to Glouberman."

"What?" I ask. "What are you talking about?"

"I got a call from the school district. It's a long story. But the short version is that the district learned we were living at your great-aunt's house. And her house isn't in the school district."

"So?"

"So if you're not in the district, you can't go to the school."

"Can't go to Glouberman?" I ask.

"Nope," she says.

"But I can go today," I shoot back. "I can certainly go one more day."

"Nope," she answers. "You can't. As of this morning, you're officially unenrolled."

"WHAT?" I shout.

"You don't have to go to school," she says. "At least until I can figure out our options."

"BUT I HAVE TO GO TO GLOUBERMAN!" I yell.

"Timmy," she says. "You can't."

"I MUST!"

"I don't understand," she says. "I thought you'd be thrilled. You hate school. Particularly that place. All you did was complain. Complain about the students, complain about—"

But I hear nothing.

Nothing but the sound of a contest I now cannot enter.

A prize I cannot win.

A universe that is collapsing.

Collapsing because of an address.

Because someone somewhere learned where I lived and felt compelled to report it to someone else.

Because that is the way the world works.

And so I lose my head.

"I GOT MYSELF KICKED OUT OF MY OLD SCHOOL FOR THIS?"

And I see my mother's face change.

From understanding.

To confusion.

To shock.

To fury.

And I limp off as fast as I can.

Out the bathroom door.

Through the house.

Through the solarium.

Into the yard.

To atop my wounded elephant.

Where I want to yell at the world.

At Carl Kobalinski.

At Alexander Scrimshaw.

At Rollo Tookus.

At Glouberman Academy.

And yet I don't.

Because I see a face.

Just over the fence.

And yell the only thing I can.

"SHENANIGANS ABOUND!"

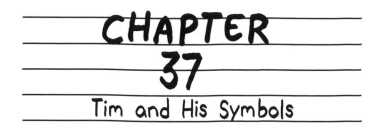

CHAPTER
37

Tim and His Symbols

"What is it?" asks the woman in the leather chair.

"It's the Tube O' Terror," I explain, pointing at my drawing. "And through corruption and deceit, it has ceased to function."

"And what's that swollen part of it?"

"That is cloggage," I say.

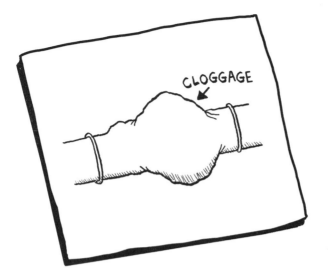

"Caused by a polar bear," I continue. "A polar bear who was too plump to ride. But who, through bribery and shenanigans, was permitted to slide."

"I think that's probably enough for today, Timmy."

"And now I must suffer for it, Dr. Dundledorf. Trapped in a waterlogged tube behind a polar bear. Because that is how the world works. In case you didn't know."

"Oh, Timmy, when you talk like that, I feel like you're making so little progress."

She smiles and gets up to leave.

"The waterslide drawing is a metaphor, Dr. Dundledorf. An analogy. A symbolic tale. I can explain it more fully if you'd like."

But she has walked out of the office.

So I sit on the couch and stare at her diplomas.

Therapist This. Therapist That. Summa Cum Laude Something or Other.

And please don't ask me what a therapist is. Because I don't know.

All I know is that I come here on Mondays and draw pictures of waterslides.

And try to explain the world to her.

Unsuccessfully.

Then I think she gets paid.

If so, it's quite a racket. One I'd like in on if I ever diversify out of the detective business.

But for now I must sit.

Because of my mother.

Yes, the very same mother who responded so well when I first got kicked out of school responded less well when she found out I did it on purpose.

"I blamed myself for everything, Timmy! *Everything!* Your bad behavior! Your drop in grades! Only to find out that you were *trying* to get kicked out. All for a stupid detective contest."

And she's right.

It was stupid.

Stupid and unfair and rigged and unwinnable.

"And if those are your priorities," she added, "and you think a children's detective contest is worth jeopardizing your entire academic future—then you need *help*."

And so here I sit.

In a therapist's office.

Defeated by an unholy alliance of Principal Scrimshaw, Glouberman Academy, and the Worldwide Enemy of Da Goodness In Everything.

← Her again

And when the winner of the detective contest is announced at this Saturday's dance, it will be the Wedgie who takes home the prize.

Not through merit or brains or hard work or skill.

But the sheer power of shenanigans.

"You ready, Timmy?" asks Dr. Dundledorf from the hallway outside her office. "Your mom's in the car, waiting for you."

So I get up to leave. But pause as I pass my
therapist in the hall.

"Do *you* think the world is fair, Dr.
Dundledorf?"

"I do, Timmy. Not all the time. But most
of the time."

I smile and nod at my therapist.

And am certain of only one thing.

She's making so little progress.

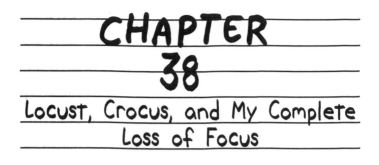

CHAPTER 38

Locust, Crocus, and My Complete Loss of Focus

For me, there is only one thing worse than leaving home for school.

And that is staying home for school.

"I don't want to be homeschooled," I complain to my mother.

"Too bad," she says, holding my math book.

"Well, what happens if you get a job?" I ask.

"I don't know, Timmy. But right now I don't have a job. So the least I can do is teach you myself."

And so we sit together for three hours a day.

And it is the longest three hours of my life.

Because during that time, I cannot day-dream. And I cannot digress. And I cannot defend the agency from its debilitating demise.

All because my mother is hovering over me like a locust on a cornstalk.

"Do you have to sit so close?" I ask.

"Focus, Timmy," says my mother.

"Little did I ever think I would long for the days of my former teacher, Frederick 'Old Man' Crocus," I tell her.

OLD MAN CROCUS

"Oh, please," says my mother. "You never liked Mr. Crocus. And he never liked you."

Which is true.

He was a teacher so traumatized by his time with me that he still sends the occasional postcard from wherever he is.

KEY WEST, FLORIDA

WISH YOU WEREN'T HERE!! HA! —CROCUS

JIMMY FAILURE

But compared to the present, that all seems like a pleasant dream.

A time when I had my whole future in front of me.

And the world was mine.

But now I've lost the world. And the globe case, too.

"Cheer up, Timmy," says my mom, picking up a stack of mail. "We're done for the day. And look. You got a letter."

So I take the letter.

And see that it is from my would-be assassin.

And I throw it away.

Because I do not care.

Not about letters.

Or assassins.

Or the work of a detective.

So good-bye to that world.

And good-bye to one more relic of my glory days.

Distinctive Scarf

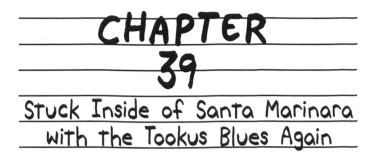

CHAPTER 39

Stuck Inside of Santa Marinara with the Tookus Blues Again

"I got it from Scrimshaw," says Rollo. "They were going to toss it."

He is holding Tapioca Me.

"That's nice of you, Rollo," I say. "But you keep it. Use it for firewood."

He leans down to talk to me.

"How long have you been under there?" he asks.

"Days. Weeks. Years," I say. "Who knows?"

"Hey, you know, you never told me what your mom and great-aunt said about the bird. Were they mad?"

"They haven't said a word."

"Well, that's weird."

"Is it?" I ask. "Maybe they feel I've suffered enough."

"Well, I heard you're getting your cast off this week," he says. "That's good news."

"Right," I say.

"And Molly Moskins won't stop asking about you. She's really crushed you're not going to the dance."

"Right," I say.

"And speaking of which, I don't know if you're still worried about it or what, but I found out everything about You-Know-Who. Turns out that's her grandparents' house next door. She was just with them because—"

"Rollo," I interrupt.

"What?" he says.

"It doesn't matter," I answer.

"C'mon," he says. "I've never seen you like this. Let's do something to cheer you up."

He looks at the tree stump.

"Let's give Tapioca Timmy a place of prominence!" he says. "How about if I put him up high on your elephant?"

"Right," I say.

"Let's do it!" cries Rollo, struggling to lift the heavy stump over his head.

Which causes Tookus to lose his balance.

And the elephant to lose his tookus.

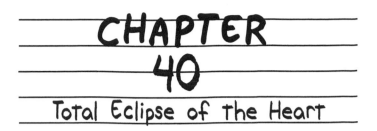

CHAPTER 40

Total Eclipse of the Heart

There is one last administrative matter to attend to.

So I attend to it.

"The disciplinary hearing into the bear will commence forthwith," I announce to the boardroom. "Will the director of ethics please read the charges?"

As the director of ethics, I read the charges.

"Count 1: Willfully eating my great-aunt's bird, Torpedo Bob."

"Are there any objections?" I ask.

But there are no hands raised.

Because the boardroom is empty.

As it has been for some time.

Because Total has quit the agency.

Upset about his treatment over the bird incident, he has decided that he no longer wants to be part of our corporation.

So I change the meeting's agenda.

And add one final motion.

"All in favor of telling the big, dumb Arctic beast that despite his big, dumb Arctic mistakes we maybe sort of wish he'd come back?"

I look around the room.

There is one hand raised.

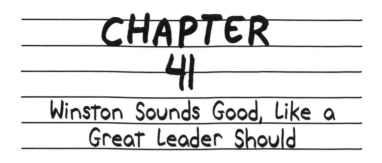

CHAPTER 41

Winston Sounds Good, Like a Great Leader Should

"When you lose hope, find it."
—Timmy Failure

I awake to the sound of a man yelling at me.

"NEVER GIVE IN! NEVER GIVE IN! NEVER, NEVER, NEVER—IN NOTHING, GREAT OR SMALL, LARGE OR PETTY— NEVER GIVE IN!"

I open one eye.

And see my great-aunt.

"What are you doing?" I ask.

"What are *you* doing?" she asks.

"I'm trying to sleep," I answer.

"And I'm playing a record," she says, pointing at a round black spinning thing.

"It's Winston Churchill," she adds. "Your buddy."

I cover my head with the pillow.

"Let me sleep," I tell her.

"Fine," she says. "You sleep. But first, I want you to hear one more speech. And this one's from me."

She turns off the record.

"Timmy, I want to tell you something I've never even told your mother. I suspected it would come up one day when she finally asked me for money. But bless her heart, she never has. So I'm going to tell you."

She pauses and smiles.

"What is it?" I ask.

"I'm pretty much broke," she says.

"Broke?" I ask. "What do you mean?"

"It means I don't have much money."

"Well, I know what *broke* means. But how can that be? You live in this great big garbanzo mansion."

"A garbanzo's a bean, Timmy. But yes, it's all a little odd. And a little confusing. But long story short, when your great-uncle died, he put everything into what's called a trust. You don't really have to understand what that is. It just means that I don't own the house. I get to live in it, sure. But it's not really mine. So I can't sell it. I can't sell anything in it."

"Why'd he do that?"

"Oh, it's a long story. But the point is that

for years, I've lived mainly off my own savings. And that's barely enough to keep up this place."

She sits on the edge of the bed.

"So that's why I don't have a new car. And that's why I don't get air-conditioning."

I think for a moment.

"And that's why your gardener said you sometimes don't pay him," I tell her.

"Bingo," she says.

"Yes. That's his name."

"No, I meant 'Bingo,' as in 'You're right.'"

"Bingo is right?"

"Never mind," she says.

I sit up in bed.

"So doesn't all that bother you?" I ask. "Him not giving you money."

"I suppose," she says. "But not nearly as much as having to serve on all those dumb boards. That, too, was a legacy of Uncle Gustav. He recommended me to fill his seat on almost every board he was on. And I stupidly accepted."

"Boring, huh?"

"Oof," she says. "You think school is dull? Try listening to a dozen people debate the dividend rate earned on a stock portfolio for three hours."

"That is a fate worse than death," I say. "So how come you're not bitter?"

"Bitter? Who has time for bitter? I have a dream. A passion. Not much different than you. Or at least the old you."

"You're talking about the Shoewheel thingies?"

SHOEWHEEL THINGIES

"Of course," she says. "The Shoewheel thingies. And I know the whole idea seems stupid and crazy, but so do most people's dreams. And I don't care. Because it's mine. It's *my* dream. And it will remain so whether or not anyone ever wants to buy a pair."

"It's so unfair," I tell her.

"What's unfair?" she asks.

"Life," I answer. "How everyone keeps you from getting what you deserve."

"Oh, Timmy."

"I'm right," I tell her. "It's the way the world works."

She sighs.

"Timmy, listen. I know you've concluded that life is unfair. And I know people are trying to tell you that you're wrong."

"And now you'll tell me that, too."

"No, Timmy, I won't. Because I think you're right."

"You do?"

"I do. I think that life is unfair. And I know that sometimes you can't control what happens to you. And I know that sometimes those things are bad. But I know something else as well."

"What?" I ask.

"I know there's one thing you *can* control. And that's how you *respond* to all those bad things."

She rises from the bed.

"You can do what you're doing now, Timmy, and give up. It's certainly the easiest way. Or, you can fight. You can fight for what you want. You can fight for what you dream."

She stares down at me.

"Now, maybe in the end you don't get what you want. But the truth, Timmy—and maybe you haven't lived enough to realize this yet—the truth is that the beauty of life, the beauty of everything, is in that fight."

She skates from the bed to the bedroom door.

And she doesn't fall.

"So do what you have to do," she says. "And I'll love you either way."

So I wait until she has left.

And rise from the bed.

And I limp.

As fast as my stupid cast will take me.

Toward the sound.

The one made by the garbage truck at the foot of my great-aunt's driveway.

Where I find the garbageman holding our garbage can.

Which I pull out of his hands.

And dump upon the grass.

And find the one thing I need.

Distinctive
Scarf↗

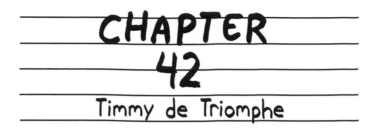

CHAPTER 42

Timmy de Triomphe

"Doesn't my Timmykins look handsomeful?" asks Molly Moskins.

"That's not a word," says Nunzio Benedici.

"And that's the third time you've asked us that, Molly," says Rollo.

"Well, I have to talk to somebody," she says. "My date isn't speaking."

Which is true.

It's A Romantic Night in Paris. I'm in a high-school gymnasium. And I'm as silent as a basketball hoop.

"Well, I, for one, think it shows tremendous sportsmanship on Timmy's part to even show up," says Molly. "I mean, he's not even *in* the contest, and yet he's here to cheer on the winner. And that shows *class*."

Rollo looks at me. I say nothing.

"I'm surprised they even let him come," says Nunzio. "Aren't you homeschooled now, Timmy?"

"That still counts as school, Nunzio," interjects Molly.

She smiles back at me. And glances at my food.

"Aren't you going to eat your frank and beans, Timmy? Even Mr. Handsomefuls have to eat."

"I don't think he's hungry," says Rollo.

"Then I'll just save it for him for later," says Molly, taking my entire dinner setting and putting it in her Hello Catty lunch box.

"Can I have his beans?" asks Nunzio.

"No," says Molly. "You'll waste them just like you did yours."

I look at Nunzio.

He has shoved most of his beans into his nose.

"I'm going for a walk," I whisper to Rollo as I stand.

"Where are you going?" asks Molly.

"He needs to use the restroom," says Rollo.

"Okay," she chirps. "But be back in time for the first dance!"

I turn and walk away from the table.

And feel like a new Timmy.

Because for the first time in many weeks,
I have no cast.

So I stroll through the gym-scented
Parisian night.

Through the Arc de Triomphe.

Under the gargoyles of Notre Dame.

To the foot of the Eiffel Tower.
Where I stare up at its peak.

And think about dreams.

And the fight for those dreams.

And the beauty of that fight.

And the room goes dark.

"*Bonjour,* students! Welcome to our first-ever all-schools dance!"

A spotlight illuminates the center of the gymnasium.

Where Superintendent Dobbs stands beneath the shadow of the Eiffel Tower.

"First off, thank you all for coming. What a wonderful turnout this is. And thank you, as well, to all you supersleuths out there who participated in our Are You a Great Detective contest! Give yourself a big round of applause."

There is scattered applause.

"And yes, as promised, tonight is the night we reveal the winner. So who among you is our very own Sherlock Holmes? And who is just an Inspector Clouseau?"

He laughs. No one else does.

"But before we get to that, I'd like to

announce a very special guest. A person we've invited to the dance tonight to read the name of the winner of our contest. And I have to tell you we are honored that he is here. Ladies and gentlemen, please put your hands together for—"

"MOLLY MOSKINS!" I yell from atop the Eiffel Tower. "*SHE* IS THE TRUE THIEF!"

A sea of faces peer upward.

"Oh, good gosh!" shouts Principal Scrimshaw, who runs under the tower and stares up at me.

"My love speaks!" cries Molly Moskins.

The gym lights flicker back on.

"What is going on?" yells Superintendent Dobbs.

"SHE HAD MOTIVE! SHE HAD OPPORTUNITY! SHE HAD—"

"Get down off that right now, Timmy!" yells Scrimshaw. "Before you break your neck!"

But before I can answer, a musical note echoes out above the Avenue des Champs-Élysées.

And all heads swivel to the Left Bank of Paris.

Where a nervous Agent F sits at the school's upright piano.

Singing and playing the same repeated note.

"*GREAT TIM-MY SEES ALL OF YOUR SINS!*"

Scrimshaw clenches his fists and begins running toward Rollo.

Rollo spots him coming, and his large round head bobs faster than it has ever bobbed before.

"*SO DO NOT TRY SHEEE-NAN-I-GANS!*" Rollo quickly sings, and runs from the piano.

Scrimshaw races after him, navigating a sea of checkered tablecloths.

One of which catches Scrimshaw's foot, causing a tabletop full of plates to hit the hard gym floor with a resounding—

CRASH!

And chaos erupts.

With kids running.

And screaming.

And blocking Scrimshaw's path.

"ROLL-O! ROLL-O! ROLL-O!" they chant as Agent F flees from Scrimshaw and darts like a French bunny around an array of Parisian landmarks.

And in the frenzy of the moment, I am able to climb down the rear of the Eiffel Tower and scramble back up with the one last prop I need.

"I AM THE SMARTEST PERSON IN THE WORLD!" I shout, prop in hand.

It is a globe I have bought at a stationery store.

And it is a powerful symbol of the contest at hand.

A symbol that will resonate among the other contestants, all of whom now realize one thing. . . .

That Timmy Failure has just solved the Biggest Case of the Millennium.

"YOU'RE MY HERO, TIMMY FAILURE!" cries the felon, Molly Moskins.

But high above the chaos, I keep my head.

For I am aware, even in this impassioned moment, that there is one grand gesture remaining.

The Banner of Greatness.

A banner sure to remind both professional and amateur alike of my place in the detective world.

But a banner now lying in a crumpled heap at the base of the Eiffel Tower.

← CRUMPLED HEAP

It was to be flown by Agent F after the playing of the Timmy Failure theme, but he has forgotten.

And he is now too busy fleeing from a fuming principal.

I begin scampering down the face of the tower to retrieve it, but am spotted by a now-vigilant Dobbs, who readies himself to capture me at the base.

I do not see him until I am halfway down.

He leaps to grab me by the ankle.

But he is unaware of my lightning-quick reflexes.

And I swing my leg wildly upward. A thread beyond his grasp.

And before he can try again, I have scrambled back up to the peak of the Eiffel Tower.

"Son, you get down here *immediately*," he barks, "or I—"

But he cannot finish.

Because his threat is interrupted by an unwieldy piece of cloth whipping rapidly past his face.

It is Agent X.

Who has infiltrated tonight's event as a dance chaperone.

"WE'LL FIGHT 'EM IN FRANCE!" she yells.

And rolls on her Boom Boom Shoewheels past the Arc de Triomphe with a grace she has never shown before.

"WE'LL FIGHT 'EM IN FRANCE!" I shout back.

And hearing my shout, Agent X cranes her head back toward the sound of my voice.

And fails to see the Parisian cross traffic that is Principal Scrimshaw and Rollo Tookus until it is too late.

"BOOM BOOM STOP! BOOM BOOM STOP!" she shouts in vain as Rollo runs face-first into the banner's broad length.

Yanking my great-aunt backward.

Where she collides with a trailing Scrimshaw.

Whose momentum powers the entire trio into the side of the gargoyle-adorned Cathedral of Notre Dame.

Causing one of the gargoyles to break off and land upon the graceless pile.

My agents in peril, I do what I must.

"I WILL SAVE YOU ALL!" I shout.

And as I do, a hand grabs my foot.

"Do not move, young man!"

It is Superintendent Dobbs. And he has climbed the Eiffel Tower to get me.

"You will wait right here until someone can get a ladder and we can get you down safely! Do you understand?"

"Yes," I answer.

And as a look of relief crosses Dobbs's sweat-drenched face, I do what only the smart-est person in the world would think to do.

I jump.

And see Dobbs's wide eyes.

And fall.

And see Molly run to catch me.

And fall.

And see Molly run into Nunzio.

And fall.

And see a gym full of shocked students.
And fall.
And see one more face.
Of the night's special guest.
Invited to announce the winner.
Now there to absorb—
my fall.

"*Bonjour,* Frederick Crocus."

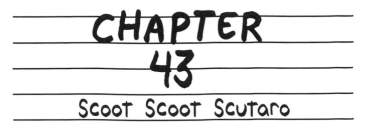

CHAPTER 43

Scoot Scoot Scutaro

When you're lying in bed with a broken *left* leg, you can either cry or finish your memoirs.

And Timmy Failure doesn't cry.

But I can't finish my memoirs.

Because Rollo Tookus won't stop talking.

"I can't believe all you broke was your leg!"

"I fall with catlike reflexes," I explain. "It's a learned survival trait."

"And I can't believe I didn't get in trouble with Scrimshaw or the school or anything!" he says.

"Will you please quiet down and let me finish my memoirs?" I ask.

"All I had to do was tell them that the whole thing was your idea, and that you *made* me do it, and that was that."

"I didn't *make* you, Rollo."

"No, but you did make me feel responsible for everything that went wrong."

I stop writing.

"It *was* your broken watch, Rollo."

"Yeah, well, the point is that now all the other kids think I'm a hero, and none of it affected my GPA!"

The poor kid. Still concerned about things that don't matter. Like *grades*.

"Listen, Rollo, I'm pleased I could give you a taste of the detective life. A break from your routine. But remember, for me, it was just another day."

"Just another day? You knocked Crocus out cold."

"Frederick Crocus knocked himself out," I answer. "Which is what I'll say should he ever file that frivolous lawsuit. That greedy charlatan may try to gouge the justice system for all it's worth."

"Then he should sue Scutaro. He's the one with all the dough."

Oh, yeah.

I forgot to tell you that part.

A kid with the highly dubious name of Scutaro Holmes "won" the detective contest and took home the five hundred dollars.

And this is what he looks like.

← SCUTARO HOLMES

From whence he came I do not know. But I have obscured his entire visage because I do not wish to give publicity to someone who is nothing more than the Wedgie's stooge.

You see, if the official account is to be given credence, Corrina Corrina (aka the Wedgie) did not even enter the detective contest.

That's right.

Did not even enter.

There are many supposed reasons for this, but let me sum them up here:

LIES, LIES, AND MORE LIES

You see, according to Rollo Tookus, the Wedgie's presence in Alexander Scrimshaw's office on that fateful day was simply to inform him that her father would be out of town for a short while. Thus, or so the story goes, she would be getting picked up from school by her grandparents, at whose house she was temporarily staying.

And because she was staying with her grandparents, she would not be near her detective office, and thus did not want to work on any cases or enter the contest.

And as if that's not enough, Rollo *also* claims that the Wedgie had nothing to do with the school finding out where I lived. That, he says, was due to my mother filling out some school form listing our address.

And if you believe all that, I have an Eiffel Tower to sell you.

So let me sum up what really happened.

The Wedgie engaged in shenanigans. The district went along at first, but after a while couldn't take the heat. And so they cracked. Convinced the Wedgie to set up a stooge. A random kid they could trot up on stage and give the cash to. Then the kid could hand the cash over to the Wedgie in some dark alley.

That way, the Wedgie could still get her dough. And more importantly, still kick back a good chunk of it to the corrupt Scrimshaw and unscrupulous Dobbs.

And no one would be the wiser.

Only she made one mistake.

She chose a kid named Scutaro Holmes. A kid with no rep in the field. And a kid who just so happens to share a last name with a very famous detective.

← THIS GUY

It is a scheme so transparent that it can only be called a farce.

But I can't talk about it anymore.

Because the Timmyline is ringing.

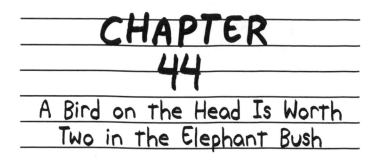

"You're lucky I agreed to meet you," I say to Nunzio Benedici. "I meet very few clients from atop my wounded elephant. It is a place of great repose."

"I just wanted to know if you solved my case," says Nunzio. "It's been a long time."

"A *long time*?" I respond. "Why, if this elephant were alive, I'd run you over right now, Nunzio. I had one leg broken by a negligent public museum. And now I have another leg broken by an old man who is incapable of catching a falling child. And you have the nerve to *lecture* me?"

"I'm sorry," says Nunzio. "I just miss Spooney Spoon."

"Fine," I tell him. "You're fortunate that I am not only skilled, but magnanimous."

"Does that mean you know what happened to Spooney Spoon?"

"Of course I know," I answer. "I'm Timmy Failure."

So I proceed to lay out all the clues.

My time spent at Glouberman. My interactions with Minnie. The spoon I saw Minnie use.

"So Minnie *did* take Spooney Spoon!" shouts Nunzio. "Just like I suspected."

I hit my elephant on the back to make him

charge over Nunzio, but the elephant does not respond.

"Will you please listen to me?" I ask. "It's bad enough you've insulted me in my place of repose."

"There's more?" he asks.

"Of course there's more."

So I take him through the night of the dance. The night of my Eiffel Tower Triumph. The night I didn't eat. The night a certain tangerine-scented girl packed up my frank and beans and put them in her Hello Catty lunch box.

"What do frank and beans have to do with anything?" asks Nunzio.

"She wanted me to *eat* those frank and beans, Nunzio."

"I don't get it."

So I draw him a picture.

Of the item she took so I could eat my frank and beans.

Nunzio stares at me.

"Just because Molly Moskins took *your* spoon doesn't mean she took *my* spoon, Timmy."

I laugh.

"Once a spoon thief, always a spoon thief, kid."

And as I say it, a bird alights upon my shoulder. As though the heavens themselves are telling Nunzio, "Timmy is special."

Until I look at the bird.

And see who it is.

And feel slightly less special.

CHAPTER 45

Sorry Seems to Be the Hardest Word to Say to a 1,500-Pound Arctic Mammal

"Mistakes were made!" I shout to my polar bear.

"BIG mistakes!" I shout. "GARBANZO mistakes!"

But Total says nothing.

"I didn't know!" I yell. "I didn't know my great-aunt had loaned her bird to some stupid charity group! I didn't know lovebirds lose their feathers! It's called *molting* or something. Who in the heck's ever heard of *that*? And how was I supposed to know you were just eating a chicken nugget when I looked at you?"

Total rolls over, his back now to me.

"Listen, if you think about it, a chicken *is* a bird," I tell him. "So technically, I wasn't really *wrong*. I was just misinformed about what *kind* of bird you were eating!"

Total gets up.

And walks out the solarium door.

I follow behind him as he crosses the backyard toward my wounded elephant.

Where he finds the shaded spot beneath and lies back down.

I stare at him for a few moments.

And see that he is not going to respond.

So I turn to walk back inside.

But stop.

"I'm sorry," I say.

And pause to steady my voice.

"I'm just sorry."

And after I say it, there is only silence.

Followed by a loud *CRUNCH* and a massive *R-I-I-I-I-I-I-I-P*.

For Total has risen to his hind legs and torn the entire bush from the ground.

And is on me in an instant, encircling me with his big, furry arms.

The safest place I can be.

Which is good.

Because there's a gardener who wants to kill me.

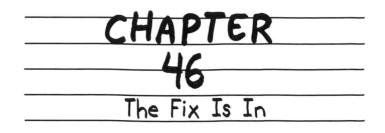

CHAPTER 46

The Fix Is In

Normally, my Eiffel Tower leap would trigger a motherly meltdown. Or perhaps another visit to Dr. Dundledorf, the poor woman who is wrong about everything.

But not this time.

Because my mother is distracted.

By our move.

That's right.

After many months of searching, my mother has gotten a job.

And we're leaving my great-aunt's house.

"And I'm not very happy about it," says Agent X, skating down the sidewalk by my side.

"Well, at least she can't teach me any-more," I say. "That was truly debilitating. And I'm assuming we'll be far enough away that I never have to see that Dundledorf again. That woman is beyond hope."

"But what about us?" asks my great-aunt.

"Rest assured," I tell her. "Your position in the agency is secure. I plan on opening a satel-lite office in your neighborhood very soon."

"You do?"

"I do. I need to keep tabs on the Wedgie's grandparents. I suspect they're covert agents."

We continue down the sidewalk in silence until we arrive at our destination.

I let go of her hand to open the museum door. She steadies herself against the facade of the building.

"You're coming in, aren't you?" I ask.

"Nope," she answers. "I'm going to say good-bye to you right here. It's as good a place as any."

"Well, it's not *good-bye* good-bye," I remind her. "It's just good-bye until we come back to visit. Or I open that office. You have a very bright future."

"That's high praise," she says. "And allow me to return the compliment."

She removes a folded envelope from her pocket.

"What's that?" I ask.

"This," she says, waving the envelope, "is my reward for sitting through one boring board meeting after another."

She hands me the envelope.

"Open it," she says.

I tear it open. And pull out a piece of paper.

THE YOUNG ENTREPRENEURS' FUND

PAY TO THE ORDER OF: TIMOTHY FAILURE $2,000

Two thousand and 00/100 DOLLARS

"What is this?" I ask.

"It's money. For you. From the Young Entrepreneurs' Fund. It's a group that helps kids start their own business. I'd know more, but I never pay attention in meetings."

I stare at the check. It is the most money I have ever seen in my life. And it is more than I ever could have won in the contest.

"I don't know what to say."

"Say good-bye," she says. "And nothing weepy. We're detectives, you know."

I hold out my arms to hug her.

But she shakes her head.

"You'll knock me over. Help me sit down first."

So I do.

And there I say good-bye to Agent X.

"And one more thing," she says as I walk toward the museum door.

I stop and turn.

"Your friend Rollo helped me."

"Helped you with what?"

"With a project," she says. "He's a good guy. Take care of him."

I watch as she starts to skate off. Each step a peril.

"Get in there," she says. "Before I fall and ruin this beautiful good-bye."

I turn to walk into the museum.

And am greeted at the door by the woman in the checkered vest.

"So that's your great-aunt, huh?" she says.

"You know her?" I ask.

"Nope," she says. "But I know she's on some community foundation something or other. One that apparently gives an awful lot of money to museums."

"And how do you know all that?"

"Because I'm almost as smart as you, kid. Now, are you gonna go in?"

So I hand her my money.

But she doesn't take it.

"Free," she says. "Today only."

So I enter the museum.

And take my usual path through the biggest, the baddest, the fattest, and the fastest.

And the smartest.

Fixed at last.

CHAPTER 47

It's All Downhill from Here

"Did you ever figure out who was sending you all those letters?" says Rollo Tookus, standing next to me atop the highest hill in Santa Marinara. "Because if you didn't, I could probably help."

"Great," I answer. "Is it amateur hour again?"

"Well, it's pretty obvious," he says. "And since you accuse Molly Moskins of every other crime, I thought for sure you'd figure this one out."

"It is not my fault that Molly Moskins has chosen a life of crime. But yes, I figured it out."

"You did?"

"Yes," I answer. "After I retrieved the assassin's last letter. The one I had thrown away."

"And what finally tipped you off?"

"Another sticky note at the bottom of the page. Like the one that said the assassin enjoyed M&M's."

"M&M's?" he asks.

"Never mind," I tell him. "The point is that this time the person made it somewhat clear what the MM represented."

"So you finally know who it is?" asks Rollo.

"I do."

"And are you going to try to arrest her again?"

"Her?" I answer. "Minnie the Magnificent is a *guy*."

"Minnie the Magnificent?" shouts Rollo.

"Nunzio Benedici's cousin," I answer. "He knew that Nunzio had put me on his trail. And he wanted me gone. Thus, the assassination attempt."

"I give up," says Rollo.

"You should," I answer. "You're an amateur and you get everything wrong. Now, are you going to go down this hill or not?"

I stare down at his Boom Boom Shoewheels.

"I really don't think I should do this, Timmy."

"You have to. You were her very first customer and she was so thrilled and—"

"You *made* me buy them. I didn't—"

"And," I say, holding up my index finger, "I think she'd be very disappointed if you weren't willing to use them."

"Great," he says. "So I'm the crash-test dummy. And what about you?"

"Don't be absurd, Rollo. I have a severely broken limb."

"And now you want *me* to have one?"

"Agent F, I made you an honorary member of my agency for a *reason*. Because you showed great bravery on the night of my Eiffel Tower Triumph. Please don't make a fool of me by showing cowardice here."

"I'll think about it," he says. "Can I at least have a last meal?"

"Fine," I say, grabbing a chicken nugget I'd been saving for Total.

Who smells the chicken nugget.

And lunges for it.

Causing me to yank the chicken nugget away from him.

And my arm to hit the back of Rollo.

Who begins rolling down the hill.

"NOOOOOOOOOOOO!" yells a rapidly receding Rollo.

Who is soon far beyond my grasp.

Causing me to turn quickly back to my polar bear.

And say the one thing he needs to hear.

"*Now* look what you've done."

Coming this fall!

Timmy's next adventure!

On sale November 2014
wherever fine books are sold!

 More Greatness